BEN BROOKS

THE GREATEST INVENTOR

Quercus

QUERCUS CHILDREN'S BOOKS

First published in Great Britain in 2020 by Hodder & Stoughton

This paperback edition published in 2021

1 3 5 7 9 10 8 6 4 2

Text copyright © Ben Brooks, 2020

Illustrations copyright © George Ermos, 2020

The moral rights of the author and illustrator have been asserted.

*All characters and events in this publication, other than those clearly in
the public domain, are fictitious and any resemblance to real persons,
living or dead, is purely coincidental.*

A CIP catalogue record for this book is available from the British Library.

ISBN 978 1 786 54114 7

Typeset in Minion Pro

Printed and bound in Great Britain by Clays Ltd, Elcograf S.p.A.

The paper and board used in this book are made from wood
from responsible sources.

MIX
Paper from
responsible sources
FSC® C104740

Quercus Children's Books
An imprint of Hachette Children's Group
Part of Hodder & Stoughton Limited
Carmelite House
50 Victoria Embankment
London EC4Y 0DZ

An Hachette UK Company
www.hachette.co.uk

www.hachettechildrens.co.uk

PROLOGUE

S ome months ago, I went to a house in the middle of nowhere to try to write a book for children. The house was big and old and came with a family of mice who lived in the walls. It was in a small village in Finland.

Every few days, my friend Felix would call to check how things were going. You would like Felix – he's very tall and frequently steals chips from other people's plates.

'How's the book?' he'd say.

'Oh,' I'd say. 'It's going wonderfully.'

Actually, it was going nowhere. I spent almost every hour of every day playing on my phone or the computer. Some days I played solitaire or poker. Other days I scrolled through pictures of friends and ex-friends and kittens and unusual pizzas.

All of that time spent not-writing made me unhappy. A grumbling grey raincloud followed me everywhere. As I stood waiting for the kettle to boil, drops of water fell on my head. While cutting spring onions for a salad, thunder crashed between my ears. I couldn't seem to drag myself away from the computer. I couldn't focus on anything for longer than three minutes and it felt like my brain was melting.

Eventually, a month had passed and I had no book to show for it. Felix called and asked how things were going.

'There's no book,' I admitted, feeling miserable. 'I've done absolutely nothing.'

He sighed. 'You know what you should do,' Felix said. 'You should go outside.'

Grumbling, I put on some fur-lined boots and a heavy coat, and headed off into the snowy woods behind the big old house. I wasn't heading anywhere in particular, I just wanted to get away from the phone and computer and try to clear my head.

But winter in Finland is very dark. The sun only shows its face for an hour or two each day, never managing to melt the metre of snow that lies on top of everything. Forty minutes into my walk, everything turned completely black. I had no idea where I was. I had no torch, no phone, no food and no plan.

I shouted and my voice rang out in the darkness.

'Hello?' I called. 'Is anyone there? I come from a different country and I'm an idiot and now I'm lost!'

There was no reply.

Panicking, I sat down in the snow and tried to catch my breath. When would people come looking? Would anyone? No one knew I'd been stupid enough to wander off alone into an unfamiliar forest. Secretly, I blamed Felix. If he hadn't called and made me feel so bad for not having written anything, I wouldn't have gone stomping off into the wilderness.

Then I felt something pulling on my trousers.

I looked down.

It was a giant tortoise, at least the size of a go-kart, and it seemed to want me to go with it. The tortoise didn't look particularly dangerous. It looked calm and strangely wise. Not having anything else to do, I followed it through the dark woods.

We eventually came to a long, low wooden house. Its windows glowed with warm light. Firewood was stacked either side of the door and sprigs of mistletoe hung in the windows.

I knocked and a boy answered the door. He was about eleven years old, green-eyed and black-haired. The boy was dressed in a T-shirt ten sizes too big for him and holding a mug of tea. He smiled when he saw me.

'Hello,' he said. 'Do you want to come in?'

'Listen,' I told him. 'You shouldn't go inviting strangers into your house like that. I could be anyone. I could be planning to rob you.'

The boy frowned. 'Are you planning to rob me?' he said.

'No,' I told him. 'But you didn't know that.'

'Good,' he said. 'Anyway, if the tortoise trusts you, then I do too. He's a very good judge of character. Last year, he bit a woodsman and a few months later we found out the woodsman had been selling fake cheese all across Pirkanmaa.'

I shook my head and hoped that no actual robbers ever ended up this deep in the woods. What, I wondered, was fake cheese?

I took a seat by the fire and the boy made me a mug of tea. It tasted like ice cream, mango, and those nuts that look like little brains. The tea managed to chase all the coldness out of me and I was soon feeling calmer than I had in a long while.

'It's lucky he found you,' the boy said, taking the seat opposite me and pulling the giant tortoise up on to his lap. 'Snow's going to start coming down heavier tonight. Doubt you'll be able to get out till the morning.'

'Oh,' I said, not thrilled at the idea of spending an entire night with the boy and his tortoise.

4

'Why were you walking around in the woods alone? Were you looking for treasure? There's no treasure anywhere between here and Helsinki, trust me, I've checked.'

'I wasn't looking for treasure,' I said.

'Then what were you looking for?'

I shrugged. 'I was looking for some peace and quiet. I'm supposed to be writing a book but I can't focus on anything. All I end up doing is playing computer chess or watching music videos.'

'Ah,' said the boy, 'I think I know what you mean.'

I doubted he did.

'Do you?'

'I think so. Can I tell you a story?'

I sighed. Whenever people find out you're a writer, they always want to tell you stories, and their stories are almost always boring. 'Fine,' I said, not wanting to offend him. 'You can tell me a story.'

And this is the story that he told me.

1

Every morning, Victor was woken by a giant tortoise nibbling on his little toe. The name of the tortoise was Saint Oswald. The name of the village in which Victor lived was Rainwater and it sat at the bottom of a valley, surrounded by three snow-capped mountains and one dark forest.

Together, the boy and his tortoise would run out of the house and race to the top of the smallest mountain. Mostly Victor would win, though Saint Oswald was much faster than others of his kind. They would always arrive at the top just in time to watch the sun rise out of the horizon, wrapping its yellow arms around the hills and breathing warmth into the towns and villages that nestled amongst them.

It was time Victor treasured because it was so quiet, and in that quiet he could be alone with his thoughts. Once the village was awake, quiet was a hard thing to find.

The days in Rainwater were long and physical. Villagers were busy mending and making, sharing and squawking, dragging ploughs and digging ditches, chasing birds off their crops into the sky. There was always something that needed to be done.

In the warm months, crops were looked after and animals were taken out to graze.

Once the snow had fallen and settled, everyone turned to indoor work: preserving foods, spinning cloth, or making tools and trinkets that could be sold to travelling traders.

For Victor, it always felt like life was something that happened outside of Rainwater. Life happened beyond the mountains and the woods, in sprawling, smoky towns packed with people. Life did not happen in the cow shed, nor on the village green.

'Don't you want to go somewhere else?' he'd ask the other kids, when they'd doze around the great oak on summer afternoons. 'Somewhere big and strange and full of new people?'

The other kids would wrinkle their noses. 'What for?' they'd say. 'We wouldn't know anyone and anyway, where would we sleep?'

Victor would sigh and shuffle off with Saint Oswald.

He learned not to share these ideas with his parents

either. Whenever he did, the response was always the same: 'Son,' they'd say, 'we may work hard here, but we work hard for ourselves, and not to make some rich person even richer. We own our ploughs, we own our land, we own our animals, and there's very few folk this side of the sea that could say the same.'

Victor didn't see what was so exciting about owning your own plough. If he had one, he'd have happily sold it for a horse so that he could set off for a grand and bustling city. Or at least he would have done if his parents had let him.

*

Our story begins one morning in early spring, with dew still glittering on the fields.

As usual, Victor was woken by Saint Oswald nipping at his feet.

'Get off, Oz,' he moaned, kicking out.

'*Uk, uk,*' said Saint Oswald.

The tortoise launched itself off the bed.

Half of the time, Saint Oswald landed on his feet and happily scurried through to the kitchen for several breakfast marshmallows. The other half of the time, Saint Oswald landed on his back, and was forced to wait for Victor to get up and turn him over.

They left the house without Victor even pausing for a

glass of water and didn't stop moving until they'd reached the summit of the smallest mountain. They always rushed in the mornings. If they ever missed a sunrise, Victor would sulk for the rest of the day. The sunrise anchored him; it made him feel like part of something far bigger and more interesting than himself.

'There she is,' Victor said, as the sun pushed up into a smudgy grey morning.

He sighed, closed his eyes, and took deep breaths.

What would he do today? he wondered. It depended what kind of mood Mum was in. Perhaps he would be told to unstitch thistles from the wheat field. Maybe he would be made to gut and clean a catch of fish that were waiting in the icebox. Or he might be told to fetch water from the well, which wasn't the worst job in the world because you could stretch it out as long as you wanted. He might also be asked to chop wood, which actually was the worst job in the world because Mum could watch from the kitchen and tut if you sat down to catch your breath.

Over the years, Victor had asked his parents for books, instruments and models. Each time he'd been turned down.

'Will they keep us warm in the winter?' his dad would ask, as though it was the most preposterous suggestion he'd ever heard. 'Can we eat them? Will they help us to bring in the harvest?'

Unless an object had a very clear and practical use, his parents saw no point in them all. It was a view shared by most of the adults in Rainwater. There were no crowded bookshelves in the village, no burnished trumpets, and no boxes of marbles or dominos. There were only tools and other tools to fix them with.

Victor felt a nip at his ankle. The giant tortoise had caught the fabric of Victor's trousers in his beak and was pulling.

'What is it?' he asked impatiently.

Saint Oswald kept tugging on his trousers.

Annoyed, Victor opened his eyes. He glared at his pet tortoise. What was Oz trying to tell him?

And then he saw it.

In the distance, moving down the winding paths cut into the mountainside, was a wooden wagon. It was difficult to make out much detail, but the wagon clearly belonged to a pedlar, rather than a pilgrim or a woodsman.

Pedlars like this only passed through the village once or twice a year. They brought with them strange new inventions from the cities, potent medicines, the seeds of newly discovered crops, and indestructible clothes made in factories. Sometimes, for the children, they performed puppet shows or swallowed swords or shared dark stories they'd carried with them from the other edge of the world.

Everyone welcomed the pedlars. They broke up the dull rhythm of life in Rainwater.

'A pedlar's coming!' Victor bellowed, racing down the mountain and skipping through the centre of the village with Saint Oswald on his heels. The people he passed threw up their hands in excitement.

Back at home, Victor found his mum and dad sitting at the kitchen table with steaming mugs of dandelion tea clamped between their hands.

'You've been off up that mountain,' his mum said disapprovingly. 'And I bet you didn't even pause for a glass of water or a bite to eat.'

'Sorry, Mum,' said Victor.

'Fluids!' said Victor's father. 'Fluids are essential for the body. You must always remember to top up your fluids!'

2

By the time the pedlar had come down the mountain, the entire village of Rainwater was waiting on the village green, clutching bags of grain and old coins and anything else they could spare to trade. It was nearly dusk and the sky had shifted from bright blue to moody orange.

Pigeons gossiped on thatched roofs.

Behind houses, dogs strained at their tethers.

And the wagon rumbled over the road that led into town. It clanked as it went, rattling the iron saucepans, brooms and hammers that hung from its sides on rusty nails. The wagon was shaped like a giant loaf of bread. A sheet of stained canvas decorated with maps of blue mould was stretched over its rickety wooden skeleton. A shaggy horse led the frail contraption. Hanging loosely from the side of the wagon was a faded banner that read:

SWIZWIT'S UNFATHOMABLE CREATIONS –
YOU WILL ACCUSE YOUR EYES OF LYING TO YOU!

The villagers watched as the wagon came to a halt. A green velvet curtain twitched at its entrance.

'Ladies and gentlemen,' said a voice from behind the curtain. 'Please bear with me as I prepare my wares for your perusal.'

It wasn't until the moon had risen that the velvet curtains parted. They revealed a row of glass lanterns, glowing dimly behind a small wooden podium. The pedlar stood atop the podium, dressed in an old shirt with a red handkerchief tied around his neck. In the darkness that surrounded him, crickets whistled, owls hooted and villagers gossiped amongst themselves.

'Good evening, good people,' he said. 'My name is Walter Swizwit and I am the greatest inventor ever to set foot in the land of King Marshalla. As your luck would have it, I am passing through this humble village on my way from the Deepest East to the grand and ancient city of Kaftan Minor.'

The people of Rainwater were thrilled. They murmured to each other, excited about what their visitor might have in

store. They had never met an inventor before, unless you counted Biff Rifkin, who'd once come up with a small wooden cage used to catch giant moths when they descended from the hills in the autumn. At the mention of Kaftan Minor, Victor had also perked up. It was a city he'd heard about in stories from other strangers who had passed through Rainwater and it sounded like the most exciting place imaginable. He was sure that if he ever got there, he'd find kids more like him than the ones in his hometown.

'It's true,' the inventor continued, bouncing eagerly on spindly legs that looked ready to collapse beneath his belly. 'I come to you from a distant place, where chalky cliffs meet the raging sea, scaly birds munch the smoky clouds, and great silver beasts haul themselves through the salty water. With me are three new contraptions that are sure to enrich your lives immeasurably.'

He smiled, revealing two rows of perfectly straight, gleaming teeth, and patted his belly as though he were pregnant.

'Now,' he said. 'May I have a volunteer?'

A number of hands shot into the air. Villagers bounced on their tiptoes, eager to be chosen. Everyone wanted to be the first to experience whatever their visitor had to offer.

Finally, Walter Swizwit selected Miss Sprocket, who

bustled up on to the stage inside the wagon. She stood excitedly in her muddied jumpsuit, coarse hands raised above her head.

'Madam,' said the inventor. 'I am about to pass you a most ingenious piece of new-fangled technology. You may be taken aback at first, but do not fear, it is there to help.'

The inventor produced a burlap sack and sank one arm into it. 'Ladies and gentlemen, I present to you . . . the Mirror of Emit Tsol.'

With a flourish, he pulled out a large, shimmery disc of metal, which he passed to Miss Sprocket.

'Please,' he told her. 'Take a careful look into this.'

Miss Sprocket held the disc up before her face.

She raised one eyebrow.

And opened her mouth.

Closed her mouth.

And flared her nostrils.

'What do you see?' asked the inventor eagerly.

Miss Sprocket peered closer.

And closer.

And closer.

Until the nose of her reflection in the metal disc touched her real nose.

'Well?' urged the inventor.

'I think it's me,' said Miss Sprocket. 'Although I couldn't tell you for sure. I've seen myself a couple o' times, in the duck pond.' She moved her face away from the mirror and wrinkled her nose. 'What's the point in that?'

'That's reflecting,' shouted one of the villagers. 'Same as a bucket of water does. Just because we live in the countryside, doesn't make us idiots.'

'What do we need reflecting for anyways?' asked Miss Sprocket.

'Well,' said the inventor. 'To see how you look.'

'Why would we need to see how we look?'

'So you can make yourselves look better.'

The villagers of Rainwater grumbled about this, upset by the suggestion that there was something wrong with how they looked already. Miss Sprocket tossed the mirror to Walter Swizwit, who dropped it, and watched with horror as it shattered into a thousand glinting pieces around his feet.

'That's seven years' bad luck,' muttered the inventor, patting his belly nervously.

'Yeah?' said an unimpressed Miss Sprocket. 'Who said?'

She took her place back amongst the crowd of villagers.

'Perhaps the divine mirror was not for you,' said Walter Swizwit, trying not to appear flustered. 'But I have no doubt my next creation will transform all of your lives.'

The villagers were not convinced. They had become restless and irritable and impatient with their visitor. Victor, on the other hand, wanted to hear everything and anything the inventor had to say. He didn't mind that the inventions seemed useless. He wanted to hear more about Kaftan Minor.

Theatrically, Walter Swizwit sank his hand into the bag once more and came out with what looked to be a pair of wooden binoculars. The device resembled a pair of chunky glasses fitted on to an oblong box, so that whoever put the spectacles on would see only the insides of the box.

No one had any idea what it could be for.

'This,' the inventor said, 'is a Greengrass Stereoscope. The very first of its kind, capable of providing an experience that is sure to be life-changing. Who would like to try it?'

People were less keen to volunteer this time. Their hopes for what the inventor might show them were fading rapidly. Hurriedly, Walter Swizwit called up a boy named Pockets Morgan and thrust the device between his hands. 'Have a look in there,' he told the boy.

Pockets Morgan pushed the device against his eyes and let out a chirp of surprise.

'Well?' said the inventor. 'What do you see?'

'It's people,' Pockets Morgan said. 'I can see people.'

'Yes,' said Walter Swizwit. 'And what are those people doing?'

'They're running around on a beach holding ice cream.'

'And?'

'They're having more fun than I am.'

'Isn't it wonderful?'

'No,' said Pockets Morgan, lowering the stereoscope from his face. 'Now I want to be on a beach and I'm stuck here in this stupid village.'

'Watch your tongue!' shouted Pockets Morgan's father from the crowd. 'This is a perfectly decent village filled with perfectly decent people!'

'But look,' said the inventor. 'Now you've got dreams, ambition, ideas about where you'd like to be. Now you know what the world has to offer and you'll stop at nothing to get it.'

Victor wished that he'd been chosen to look through the Greengrass Stereoscope.

Pockets Morgan looked sadly around at the villagers. 'Why is there no beach? Why isn't there any ice cream?'

His father dragged him out of the wagon.

'We don't have time to watch other people having fun,' he said. 'We have things to do. Fields to plough, cows to milk, children to bath.'

'Who is this man anyway?' someone shouted.

'Let's go home, he's obviously a lunatic.'

'Wait!' called the inventor. 'I have one more invention for you all, and it is sure to astound, amaze and inspire.'

'You said that last time,' pointed out Victor's mother. 'And then you pulled out wooden binoculars and said the world had more to offer than our village.'

'Well, I've saved the best for last,' promised the inventor. 'You'll see. Prepare yourselves for . . . the Moveable World.'

They watched with their arms crossed as the inventor pulled a series of objects out of his bag and arranged them on the podium.

First came a wooden barn, about the size of a shoebox. One side of the barn swung open to reveal its inside, which was set out exactly like a real barn, with feeding troughs, pens and bales of hay.

Next came the animals. Pigs, horses, goats and sheep, each no bigger than a thumb, and all capable of making life-like sounds and leaving behind life-like deposits.

Finally, the inventor brought out a farmer, and placed him proudly beside the animals.

The villagers muttered loudly to each other.

'This,' said the inventor, gesturing grandly with his arms, 'is a miniature farm, that you can operate almost exactly as if it were an actual real-life farm.'

The villagers of Rainwater fell silent.

'Why would we want to do that?' someone asked.

'Because,' said the travelling salesman, 'it's fun.'

At that, the villagers burst out laughing. They bent in half and slapped their knees and roared until they couldn't breathe. Why would it be any fun to run a tiny farm? They already ran normal-sized farms and that could hardly be called fun. Fulfilling, perhaps, satisfying maybe, but certainly not fun.

'Now that,' said someone, 'was funny.'

As they left, a few people hurled rotten vegetables, while others invented insults and showered the inventor with them. Walter Swizwit stood beside his wagon, turning a deep, dark shade of red. He ground his teeth and stamped his feet and patted his belly like someone trying to put out a fire.

The villagers returned to their homes and continued tittering to themselves about what they'd seen.

Crusty heels of bread and cauldrons of chicken soup were warmed and shared. If he hadn't brought any useful inventions, they agreed, he'd at least given them a chuckle. Laughter in Rainwater was in short supply. Now it was time to think about the morning and the challenges it would bring. There were scarecrows that needed new hats, horses that needed new shoes.

Only Victor didn't laugh. He was too disappointed to find it funny. Seeing that wagon roll down the mountainside, he'd hoped for a glimpse into the wider world. Instead, all it had brought were cheap tricks.

3

The inventor drew the velvet curtains across his wagon and sat in the darkness seething, surrounded by his inventions. 'How dare they laugh!' he muttered to himself. 'Those slow-minded, shovel-handed, straw-brained farm-folk. How dare they mock me!'

They are only savages, he told himself, *simple people from the country who can't grasp anything more exciting than a wooden spoon.* But those savages were getting in the way of his plans. It was absolutely necessary that he made as much gold as possible. If he didn't, he would fail.

And he couldn't afford to fail.

Everyone else between this wretched valley and the Eastern Ocean had bought the inventions, so what made the villagers of Rainwater think they were so special?

He pictured the villagers in their homes, laughing about him. The more he thought, the angrier he got.

'Well,' the inventor said to himself, 'not a single villager in this reeking hamlet will be laughing come morning, I'll see to that.'

And he crept out of his old wagon and snuck among the huts, hopping between pools of darkness.

He knew what he was looking for and soon he found it.

In the centre of the village of Rainwater was a well so deep that folk claimed if you fell into it, you'd fall for three days. Every morning the villagers drew water from it for their breakfast teas. Every morning, each villager drank at least three cups of some kind of tea. Theirs was a community built on tea. There were special teas for funerals, teas for birthdays, teas for Tuesdays and Fridays and the days of first and last snow.

Standing over that deep well, the inventor unfolded a handkerchief and shook a sprinkling of silver dust into its water. He cackled to himself. 'That should sort them out,' he whispered.

On the village green, he closed the curtains over his wagon and climbed up to the front. He took the reins of his horse and urged her on.

'On you go, girl,' he told the horse, adjusting the black and white photograph of his sister that he kept tucked into his jacket pocket. 'We've plenty more places to see yet,

and I'm sure we'll get a warmer welcome than ever we
got here.'

4

The next morning, Victor was woken again by Saint Oswald nipping at his feet. He nudged the animal away and rolled over.

'*Uk, uk,*' said Saint Oswald, launching himself off the bed. The giant tortoise landed on his back and was forced to wait for the boy to get up and right him.

Victor was still halfway through a dream. He watched the bald and roaring monster advance, turned to run, and blinked his eyes open.

'I was dreaming,' he told the ceiling. 'It was just a dream.'

Victor climbed out of bed, picked up Saint Oswald, pulled on some dirty clothes from the floor and headed outside.

Together they raced to their normal spot at the top of the smallest mountain.

The sun rose, soft and warm on the slopes of the valley. Carpets of dew sparkled in the light.

Victor hoped that another wagon was about to come rumbling into view. It didn't, of course. He knew it could be months, even years before another pedlar stopped by. What was it like in the Deepest East? Was there really an ocean? And did it really reach to the end of the world? Did the people play violins and whistles and read from thick old books filled with the kinds of stories that the strangers who had passed through Rainwater told? Surely, he thought, the people in the cities would make sense to him and he would make sense to them.

He lingered a little longer than usual on the top of the mountain, lost in his thoughts.

'We'd better go, Oz,' he said, finally. 'I'm sure Mum's written our list of chores already.'

They hurried down the mountain.

Before they reached the bottom, Victor slowed his pace.

Something was wrong.

Rather than the usual morning bustle, the village streets were deserted. Not a single person could be seen out of their hut. This had never happened before. Almost everyone would be awake by the time Victor returned from the mountain, even if most of them chose to ignore him entirely. Could they all just be sleeping in?

Cautiously, Victor pushed open the door to his house.

He saw his mum and dad lying on the kitchen floor, balled up like new-born babies. They both appeared to be in great pain, squawking like frightened birds.

'Don't drink the water!' his father bellowed from below the kitchen table. 'It's poisoned!'

'It's true,' whimpered his mother. 'We can barely move and our stomachs feel like explosions. Your father's already chucked up both his lungs.'

Victor wrinkled his nose. He helped his parents get up and led them through to their bedroom. They collapsed into bed. Sweat ran from their heads and their hands trembled. Their eyes were threaded with red and the skin of their cheeks was turning yellow.

'Did the inventor do this?' Victor asked. 'Did he do this to you because no one bought his stupid inventions?'

'Of course!' shouted his father. 'Who else! The impish charlatan has ruined us!'

'Go and see the Great Aunt,' his mother insisted. 'Ask for medicine. She'll know what to do.'

Victor didn't want to leave his parents in that state, but he had no other choice.

The Great Aunt was the oldest woman in the village. She could speak to woodlice, warn away fire and make promises to the rain. She could diagnose the sick just by staring into their eyes and then brew potions from plants that cured them. Some kids said she was as old as the youngest star, others said she was even older than that. The Great Aunt wore thick silver rings on her fingers and beads of polished glass in her hair.

Victor knocked at the Great Aunt's door but got no reply. He entered, calling out 'Hello?' and wandering from room to room until he found her curled up in bed, moaning.

'Boy,' she said, holding out a dented tin cup. 'Fetch me a cup of water from the stream – that should still be safe at least.'

He ran, there and back.

Then he gave the tin cup to the Great Aunt and watched her glug from it.

'Are you okay?' Victor said. 'Has the inventor really poisoned everyone? Can you fix it?'

'This is no poisoning,' said the Great Aunt. 'It's something far worse. Some strange magic that is here to stay, unless a cure is found. A man with that kind of malice in him would not inflict only a passing unpleasantness. This is not something I can fix, I am afraid.'

'Then how do I help Mum and Dad?'

The Great Aunt tried to sit up and failed. She slumped, tangled in her bedsheets like a stringless puppet. 'Are you the only one unaffected?' she asked.

Victor nodded. 'Me and Saint Oswald,' he said. 'Or at least I haven't seen anyone else who's okay.'

'Then you two shall have to go,' said the Great Aunt. 'You shall have to pursue the inventor that inflicted this on us and find a way to undo it all.'

'But how am I supposed to do that?'

The Great Aunt ignored his question. 'First,' she said, 'you shall have to make certain arrangements. In this condition, no one will be able to fetch water or make food. Everything must be within reach if we are to survive until you return. Can you do that?'

'I'll try my best.'

For the next week, Victor worked to arrange things so that every villager of Rainwater would have enough food and water to last them a month. He carted vats of water down from streams in the hills, carried jars of preserved vegetables up from basements, and brought slabs of dried meat down from lofts. Saint Oswald was made to drag barrels of pickled carrot between houses. Anything even close to being ripe or fully grown was plucked from its tree, vine or bush and stacked in heaps around the beds. All of the horses had fallen sick from the water, along with the humans, which meant there was no one to help with the work.

By the end of the week, Victor was thoroughly exhausted. And his adventure hadn't even started.

'Now be warned,' the Great Aunt told him. 'The world beyond our village is a cruel one. Though you may not have realised it, you have lived in a bubble while growing up here in Rainwater.'

I did realise it, thought Victor to himself, *and I've never wanted anything more than to escape.* But as much as he'd dreamt of leaving his home, he'd never imagined it would happen like this.

The Great Aunt frowned as though she could read his mind.

'You may well think it boring here,' she said. 'But there are many things worse than boredom. After the Iron Plague swept the land, life became truly unbearable for many people.'

'The Iron Plague?' asked Victor.

'We do not teach it to you Rainwater children because there is no need. There are events of the past that can teach us, and others that can only terrify us.'

'What was it?'

The Great Aunt shuddered at the thought of it. 'The Iron Plague was an illness that arrived on a ship from a land that has long since disappeared. The plague caused all plants and animals to turn to metal and rust away to nothing in the rains that started falling and would not stop.'

'Then how did you get here?'

'The Great-Great Grandmother led us to safety. She was a wise woman with great powers. But more than power, she had courage enough to walk into the darkness.' The Great Aunt clutched her chest and let out a howl of pain. 'Now you must go,' she said. 'Before he reaches the city. If he is swallowed by the swirling masses, you may never find him.'

Victor hurried back toward his house, head humming with all the new information.

'Are you sure you'll be okay?' he asked his mother and father, watching them shifting uncomfortably in their bed. They were both suffering from fevers and cold chills and saw purple galaxies spinning across their eyes when they blinked.

'What else are we going to be?' said his father. 'We shall be okay! Of course we shall.'

'Be careful, sweetheart,' said his mother. 'Don't talk to strangers or eat strange mushrooms, don't forget your pleases and your thank yous, and when that whopping great tortoise does a poo, you pick that poo up, understand?'

Victor rolled his eyes. 'I'll clear up after him, Mum.'

'Then go,' she said. 'And good luck. We know you won't let us down.'

He bent to embrace his parents in a hug and felt unexpected tears prickling at the prospect of leaving them behind.

5

The path that led out of Rainwater was crumbling, faint and overgrown. The villagers hardly ever followed it into the dark woods – too many scary stories had been told to them as children.

Victor paused before he stepped into the shadow of the forest. It was the first time he'd gone further than the top of the smallest mountain. He had no real idea about what lay beyond their valley; all he had was a vague hope that it was more exciting that what he was leaving behind.

'This is it,' he said to Saint Oswald. 'We're finally leaving Rainwater.'

'*Uk, uk,*' said Saint Oswald.

'I know, it's not exactly how I wanted to go either. But still, what if we save everyone and we get to see Kaftan Minor.'

And on they went.

It was cool in the shade of the forest and the walking was flat and easy. Butterflies the colour of autumn afternoons flitted between trees. Deer loped around ancient ruins. Sweet droplets of sap oozed from gnarled bark.

Saint Oswald pulled a wooden cart containing their supplies: bread and cheese, vegetables, salty pucks of meat, blankets, flint to make fire, herbs for tea and small paper bags for the picking up of tortoise poo. Fortunately, the tortoise only pooed once per day. Unfortunately, there was nothing to do with the poo but load it on to the cart and pray that they'd eventually come to a compost heap.

Victor also carried with him a vague map that had been drawn by the Great Aunt. The path, the map claimed, led first to the village of Moonwald – after that, all he could really make out were dark squiggles. If the inventor wasn't in Moonwald, Victor had no idea what he'd do. At least, he reasoned, the further they were from Rainwater, the closer they would be to a city.

As they walked deeper into the woods, Victor began to spot posters nailed to the trunks of trees. They featured sketches of the inventor's creations being used by smiling people. The posters also had scribbled words written under the pictures that read:

THE MIRROR OF EMIT TSOL
SEE YOURSELF AS OTHERS DO

THE GREENGRASS STEREOSCOPE
YOU DON'T WANT TO MISS OUT ON ALL THE FUN, DO YOU?

THE MOVEABLE WORLD
FINALLY, SOMETHING YOU CAN CONTROL!

He tore down as many of the posters as he could.

Once he realised that they weren't going to reach Moonwald before nightfall, Victor began looking for a place to set up camp. There wasn't much of a choice. There were trees and trees, the narrow path and more trees.

'Here's as good as anywhere,' he soon said, pointing to a patch of bare ground between two spindly oaks.

Victor tied a length of rope between two trees, slung a tarpaulin over it, and weighed each side down with a selection of nearby rocks. It wasn't much of a tent, but it would do.

He lit a fire.

In the flames, he heated water and made tea from nettles,

then warmed up a jar of vinegary onions and cut a few slices of thick black bread. The boy and his tortoise ate quietly as the fire crackled and moths swooped across the light.

Unfamiliar sounds echoed through the depths of the forest.

Victor shivered, unpleasant thoughts crowding him in the silence.

'I wish we could have taken a horse,' he lamented. 'What if the inventor is farther than Moonwald already? How would we find him?'

'*Uk, uk,*' said Saint Oswald.

'Even if we do catch him, I'm not sure what we'd do. Why would he help us?'

'*Uk,*' said Saint Oswald.

'You're being silly,' said Victor. 'I couldn't fight a horsefly.'

Saint Oswald didn't know what to say to that. They both crawled into the tent and lay side by side as the woods shrieked and hollered around them.

A few moments later, it started to rain. A few moments after that, it started to pour. Water rushed in torrents through the canopy, snapping branches and stripping the leaves off twigs. The solid ground turned to slurry. The bugs and the birds fell silent as they rushed to find shelter from the deluge.

'What do we do?' Victor asked Saint Oswald, his voice muffled by the downpour.

'*Uk, uk, uk,*' said the tortoise.

'No, I know we can't stop it. But it's coming through the tent.'

Victor wrapped his arms around the animal's shell. Water splashed off their heads and soaked into their blankets. The canvas ceiling of the tent began to sink with the weight of the water it was collecting. Soon enough, it was touching Victor's nose, and he pushed against the fabric until some of the water sloshed to the ground.

'I'm not sure I like this adventure,' he whispered.

The tortoise said nothing.

In that strange and scary place, it felt like sleep would never come, until the hard work of the last week caught up with them and tiredness fell like a duvet. The last thing Victor thought before he fell asleep was, *I miss my bed.*

6

Dawn had transformed the forest. It was no longer the dark woods, but a glowing green jungle. The thick leaves were now panes of stained glass that spread sunlight in curious patterns over the mossy floor. Already most of the rain had evaporated, leaving behind only a few crystals of clear water clinging to the tips of twigs.

And the spooky sounds were gone too, replaced by birdsong and the bubbling of running water.

Victor climbed out of the tent, yawning and stretching, feeling exhausted but far less terrified than he had done the previous night.

And then he opened his eyes.

The cart that had been piled high with their supplies was completely empty. Where the parcels of meat and jars of pickled vegetables had been stashed, there was only bare wood, decorated with deep claw marks. It looked as though they'd been robbed by a large and fearsome beast.

'No!' Victor cried, falling to his knees. 'It's all gone.' He buried his head in his hands. 'We don't know where we're going and now we have no food to get there with. We might as well go home.' He felt the tortoise nip at his ankle and sighed. 'Yes, I know, I know. If we don't save Mum and Dad and the whole village then no one else will.'

'*Uk*,' said Saint Oswald.

'You're right,' said Victor, trying his best to raise a smile. 'We might even get to see a city too. If we don't get completely lost and starve first.'

Victor plucked a few nettles from the ground and boiled them with some of the rainwater that had collected in his boots. He sipped his tea, feeling much less certain than he had when he'd set out. Reluctantly, he stood up and looked at Saint Oswald.

'I guess we'd better get moving,' said Victor.

Back up and on to the path that seemed to wander endlessly between the trees.

Victor spent the journey trying to ignore the rumbling of his belly by daydreaming of great cities. Having never seen a city, he pictured Rainwater but ten times bigger, or a hundred times bigger, or sometimes a thousand times as big. He saw buildings that climbed through clouds, and libraries, and gardens grown in glass houses.

As they walked, Victor stooped to collect the plants and flowers that he recognised from the teas they made back in Rainwater. He even found a family of mushrooms that smelled like roasted nuts. Gently, he cut them away from their roots and dropped them sadly into the empty cart, then tied the plants to Saint Oswald's back. It wasn't much but it would be enough to keep them going for a while.

'Don't let anyone eat them,' he told the tortoise.

A little after midday, they reached the village of Moonwald.

It was certainly not a city.

The settlement was built between a towering cliff and a shallow stream that ran over a bed of orange stones. A giant black hole was punched into the cliff and railway tracks ran into the darkness of it. The houses that made up the village were short and solid and built from dark stone. Stacks of firewood were piled up outside of them, along with dust-covered work boots and patched overalls. It was a place built with work in mind, a place meant for serious business and hard labour.

Victor wasn't sure whether the inhabitants of the village would welcome him. They might be suspicious, especially if they'd just encountered the same inventor that had been in Rainwater.

'Halt!' called a voice from behind a chimneypot. 'Who goes there?'

'No one,' said Victor, stopping in his tracks.

'You gotta be someone,' said the voice. 'So just tell me.'

A girl hopped off a nearby rooftop. She was dressed in shorts held up by frayed rope, wearing several scarves and

holding a bow aimed squarely at Victor's face. The girl had used dark mud to paint streaks under both of her eyes.

Victor put his hands up. 'Don't shoot,' he said.

'I'll shoot if I want to,' said the girl. 'You can't tell me what to do.'

'But I'm not a baddie.'

'I'll be the judge of that.' The girl narrowed her eyes and waved her bow threateningly.

Victor looked around him. 'Where is everyone else?'

'Inside,' the girl said.

'Don't they have jobs to do?' he asked, a sinking feeling spreading through his belly.

'Course they do,' the girl said, looking along the length of the arrow at Victor. 'This is a mining town. We unpick rubies from the depths of the deep cave and pass them on to the collectors.' Suddenly, out of nowhere, a great sadness came across the girl's face. She lowered her bow and let the arrow clatter to the ground. 'Everything changed about a week ago,' she said. 'When this idiot inventor came rolling into town on his stinking wagon.'

'That must be the same man I'm looking for!' said Victor. 'I've been trying to follow him from my village but I wasn't sure where he went.'

The girl stepped closer to Victor and slung the bow over

her back. 'What stupid thing did he sell your people?' she asked miserably.

'He didn't sell us anything. Everyone laughed at him and he poisoned our well. Now I need to track him down and find the cure. My parents are sick in bed; so is everyone else. They can't even get out to gather food or bring in water.'

'Really?' The girl clenched her fists at her sides. 'If I ever find him, I'm going to pull out his eyes and feed them to the birds.'

Victor took a step back from the girl. 'What happened when he came here?'

'He sold all the adults here shiny plates that show themselves their own dumb reflections. Since they've gotten them, all anyone wants to do is sit inside looking at themselves. From morning till night, they cut each other's hair and pluck each other's eyebrows. Worst thing is, they all refuse to go into the mine in case they get dirty. But someone has to go into the mine, otherwise when the collectors come, they'll say we're not paying our way, and they'll kick us out of our homes. So all the kids have to do the work instead.'

'Who are the collectors?'

'You don't know who the collectors are?'

Victor shook his head.

'Everything in Moonwald belongs to the collectors,' she explained. 'They own our houses and our tools and our carts. We have to pay them back. Every month, they come and take the rubies we've mined and give us food and clothes and whatever else we need. It's how things have always been.'

It sounded strange to Victor. 'Why don't you just grow your own food?' he said.

The girl stared at him like he'd just suggested filling their pants with rocks and dancing like chickens. 'Grow your own food?' she said. 'How are you supposed to do that?'

'Well,' he said. 'You put seeds in the ground and then look after them.'

'Where do we get seeds?'

'From the food,' he said. 'I think they're in the food.' Victor scratched his head. 'If everyone's supposed to be in the mine, how come you're not down there too?'

The girl stuck out her chin. 'I have asthma,' she said. 'The dust in there can trigger an attack, which means I could die. So instead it's my job to keep watch over the village, which I was doing a good job of until you came along.'

The girl was acting tough but her eyes gave her away. She wasn't like any of the kids in Rainwater. There was something more grown-up about her. Even though she looked about Victor's age, he got the feeling she'd been alive for a lot longer than he had. The bow and arrow didn't help. None of the boys and girls in Victor's village were allowed to touch weapons, let alone learn how to use them.

'Do you always point arrows at people who come here?'

The girl nodded sadly. 'In case they come to take the rubies,' she said. 'If anyone takes anything, we get in serious trouble.'

The girl looked so upset that Victor wanted to cheer her up, though he wasn't sure what he could do to help. He couldn't sing or dance or tell any jokes, and he guessed that a hug from a stranger might feel more like an attack than anything else.

Instead, he nudged Saint Oswald forward, hoping that the tortoise might lift her spirits. The creature tootled gently toward her. How could anyone be afraid of Saint Oswald?

'I like your turtle,' the girl said.

'He's a tortoise,' said Victor, trying his best not to sound like a schoolteacher. 'Turtles go in the water and tortoises go on land.'

'That can't be right.'

'I think it is.'

She crouched and ran her hand over Saint Oswald's intricate shell. 'Well, I like him anyway.'

'*Uk, uk*,' said the tortoise.

'I'm Elena,' the girl said, standing up and sticking out her hand.

'Victor,' said Victor.

They shook hands and Victor offered to make tea, an offer which Elena readily accepted.

Victor used the flowers he'd collected to brew tea and he roasted the mushrooms over a small fire. Four cups of tea and three mushrooms later, Elena patted her belly and fell on to her back.

'So,' she said. 'What's your plan?'

'My plan for what?' asked Victor.

'When you find the inventor, how are you going to get the cure from him? Will you fight him? Threaten him? Torture him?'

'I'm not sure yet,' said Victor. 'I doubt I'll torture him.'

'He's not going to help you for free. He'll want something. Do you have any money?'

'No,' Victor admitted.

'A weapon?'

'I'm not even allowed to hold the scissors at home.'

'Some saviour you'll be. I'm sure the evil travelling inventor will happily hand over the cure just because you ask him nicely and flutter your eyelashes.'

Victor felt the hope fall out of him. Why would she say

something like that? Of course he'd find the inventor and of course he'd find out how to make everyone at home better. After all, what choice did he have?

Elena could see she'd upset Victor, as could Saint Oswald, who nibbled on the hem of his trousers. 'I'm sorry,' she said. 'I was being thoughtless. I'm sure you'll think of something.'

'I will,' said Victor. 'I'll have to.'

As the stars came out, so did the children of Moonwald. They trudged out of the mine pushing huge rail carts loaded with shining rubies.

The children looked miserable.

Their faces and hands were hidden under layers of dirt and sweat and their clothes were torn and their feet were blistered. Each step was a monumental effort.

'See?' said Elena. 'I don't know how much longer this can go on for. The kids will work themselves senseless and it still won't be enough for the collectors.'

Victor realised that he ought to ask the girl to go with him in search of the inventor. He knew he ought to but he wasn't sure he wanted to. It had always just been him and Saint Oswald and they'd gotten on just fine. The other kids in Rainwater didn't make sense to them, but they made sense to each other. So did they really need someone else coming along, especially if that someone else wanted to shoot everyone with a bow and didn't think they were capable of taking on the inventor anyway?

Victor looked out at the masses of exhausted children. He was going to help Rainwater but who would help them?

He sighed.

'You should come with me,' he said finally. 'If anyone knows how to get them away from the mirrors, it'll be him.'

And Elena agreed, because she wasn't sure what other choice she had.

7

Victor, Elena and Saint Oswald rejoined the path that led through the forest. They walked in single file, the tortoise sandwiched between them, dragging the rattling cart loaded with the very few supplies they had left.

'I should probably tell you,' said Victor. 'I have no idea where we're going.'

Elena smiled. 'I think I know. After he sold the idiotic mirrors to my parents, the inventor asked for directions to the next village. My dad told him how to get to Aeldbird.'

'Do you know the way?'

'I've never been, but I think I can remember what Dad told him.'

Like Victor, Elena had never left her village either. She was surprised and delighted to hear about the crops and the animals back in Rainwater. Victor was equally surprised to hear that all anyone in her village did was mine rubies. It sounded like a simpler way of life, he supposed, even if the work was gruelling and dull.

'What about your tortoise?' asked Elena.

'He's called Saint Oswald,' said Victor.

'Does he do anything?'

'Like what?'

'Dance?'

'I'm not sure. I don't think so.'

'Can you eat him?'

'I'd never eat him,' said Victor, horrified. 'He's my best friend.'

The mood was tense for a while after that, until Elena apologised, both to Victor and to Saint Oswald, and they both accepted the apology with a nod.

The three of them paused for a break when they came to a tree that had been struck by lightning. Its blackened trunk had fallen across the path. They helped each other up and sat for a while with their legs swinging into the bark.

A fire was started and lunch was made: Victor's recipe, consisting of dandelion heads and the last of the mushrooms. It tasted strange to Elena, until it didn't taste strange any more, and she greedily ate the tiny portion she was given before peering into the pot and frowning at its emptiness.

Saint Oswald wandered a few steps away, made a low grumbling sound, and deposited a poo on the ground.

Victor snatched a bag off the cart and leapt down to pick it up.

Elena was disgusted. 'What are you doing?' she said.

'Um,' said Victor. 'Picking up the poo.'

'Why would you pick it up?'

'My mum said I had to.'

'She said you had to carry its poo around with you?'

'Well, she said I had to clear up after it, and there's no compost heap or field to spread it on.'

Elena wrinkled her nose. 'Why would you spread it on a field?

'It helps the vegetables to grow.'

'You put poo on the vegetables?'

Victor laughed. 'Not on the vegetables, on the soil. It adds nutrients.'

'That's sick.'

'All farmers do it.'

'They do not.'

'Do too.'

'Do not.'

'Do too.'

The argument ended when they both fell into fits of

giggles. Saint Oswald watched them like an exasperated parent. Was his poo really so funny?

'What if the inventor's ten thousand miles in front of us already?' Victor asked, once they'd stopped laughing.

'Maybe he found somewhere he liked and decided to stay,' Elena said.

'Or maybe one of the villages coming up is his home,' Victor said more cheerfully.

'I guess he must have a home.'

'But if he had a home, why would he leave it to travel around selling pointless things to people?'

'Not sure,' said Elena. 'It must be making him a lot of money, though. Once the people at home got a look in those mirrors, they were pretty much willing to offer him whatever they had for them. My mum gave him all the coins she'd been saving to try to buy our house back from the collectors. I don't know how she could be so dumb.'

It was soon nightfall once again. They set up camp under a willow tree, whose branches hung down to the ground, forming a curtain that surrounded them. There was no need for tents. They stretched the blankets over the three of them, with Saint Oswald taking the middle spot.

'Elena?' Victor whispered.

'What?' she whispered back.

'What do you think it's like in a city?'

'I think it's probably like living with a hundred thousand turtles except there's no one around to clear up their poo.'

'He's a tortoise,' said Victor. 'Not a turtle.'

But she was already asleep.

In the darkness, Victor lay next to Saint Oswald, with one hand flat on his rumbling belly. He had never felt so hungry before. He'd never spent so long with someone who wasn't one of his parents either. How strange it must be to be another person, he thought, to look at the world through a different pair of eyes and think different kinds of feelings when you saw a jubjub bird or bit into a prickly pear.

He wondered what Elena thought of him.

He wondered what he thought of Elena.

She said things he couldn't understand and made him upset and angry and didn't know how to light a fire or which flowers to pick for tea. But still, for all that, there was something better about being hungry with another person than being hungry alone.

'*Uk*,' said Saint Oswald.

'I know,' said Victor. 'I was never really alone.'

8

The village of Aeldbird could be heard far sooner than it could be seen. It sounded more like a zoo than it did a human village.

'Are you sure this is the right way?' Victor asked nervously.

'It's what Dad said,' Elena insisted. 'The rightmost road leads to Aeldbird.'

Cautiously, they carried on down the track.

The closer they got to the village, the darker everything became. Branches crowded together to block out the light. Leaves turned solid. The undergrowth rose high and melted into the canopy, becoming a thick ceiling of vegetation that blocked out almost all traces of the sun.

'We must be close,' said Victor.

The sounds were almost deafening, though they still couldn't see any signs of people. It had to be nearby . . .

'Watch out!'

Elena seized Victor by the collar and yanked him backwards.

He fell on his back in the scratchy grass.

Elena was staring down at a forty-foot drop.

'I guess that's Aeldbird,' she said, pointing.

The village that appeared before them had been built deep inside a vast crater. It consisted of a number of spindly wooden houses, papered over with leaves, and a long, wall-less hall, in which hundreds of animal furs hung. The place appeared to be trying to hide itself, to keep anyone from realising it was there.

But the odd thing about the village was not the shack hung with furs, or the half-hidden houses. The odd thing about Aeldbird was the large numbers of living animals stalking its streets. There were bears lolling on their backs, wolves tumbling over each other, and rabbits bouncing between the gutters.

It was a place that had been overrun by wildlife.

Except for in one spot, on the roof of one house, where a small, red-faced boy stood, awkwardly clutching a spear to his chest. He looked exhausted, panicked, and like he'd already cried out all the tears he had in him. His shirt was tied around his head and his socks had been relocated to his hands.

Elena drew her bow and aimed it at the boy.

'What are you doing that for?' Victor whispered.

'He might attack us,' she whispered back. 'He looks mad.'

'You have to calm down. Not everyone wants to attack you.'

The boy screamed when he saw the two of them.

'Please!' he shouted, waving his arms in the air. 'Don't shoot me! I beg you. I didn't do anything and I'll taste terrible!'

'Are you going to attack us with that spear?' demanded Elena.

'I swear I won't spear you,' the boy said, looking at the weapon in his hand. 'I never speared anything before in my whole life.' As if to demonstrate, he threw the spear off his rooftop, and watched as it was shattered into splinters by a black bear. 'Whenever they go out hunting, I just hide up here. That's how come I'm stuck. I hate hunting. It gives me a rash behind the knees.'

'What kind of village is this?'

'It's a hunting village,' the boy said. 'Or it was. Now it's . . . I don't know. A hunted village. Since that man came through, everything's changed. He was really tall and he spoke really loud.'

'Did he wear a handkerchief around his neck?' Victor asked.

'And drive a broken old wagon?' added Elena.

'That was him!' the boy said. 'He came into town and sold everyone these weird wooden binoculars. If you look into them you see people just walking around having a nice time. Everyone else is glued to them. Go look in the huts and see for yourself. They're all just sitting around staring into them. Once the animals realised no one was moving, they just walked right into the village and took over. Since then they've been wandering the streets, waiting for people to come out. No one's come out yet, but they have to eventually, right? They're pulling the houses apart too, those bears. Pretty soon they'll be inside them, and they'll want revenge. We've been hunting animals ever since my great-grandfather was the size of a grape.'

The boy's lower lip trembled as if he were about to burst into tears.

'Do you think you could help me?' he said. 'I've been trapped up here a while now and my belly's rumbling and my throat feels like it could sand down a plank of wood.'

'We'll help you,' Victor shouted.

'How?' hissed Elena, pulling Victor away from the lip of the cliff.

'We need to cause some kind of distraction so that the animals leave. Then, we get him out of the crater and bring him with us to find the inventor.'

'He's coming with us?'

Victor shrugged. 'He needs help as much as we do. His parents are in trouble too. If we leave him up there, something's going to eat him sooner or later. Besides, maybe he knows where the inventor went.'

They both looked at the boy. He was still waving his arms and had started performing a kind of helpless dance.

The animals had taken notice. Several wolves howled around the foundations of the house, daring him to come down. Bears flashed their razor teeth. Rabbits twitched in anticipation.

'What's your name?' shouted Elena, through cupped hands.

'I'm Mingus,' the boy shouted back.

'Mingus, would you say you would be of use on a quest?'

'Ignore her, Mingus,' shouted Victor. 'If you could just stop dancing a second, we're going to try and get you off that roof, okay?'

9

It was not a good plan but it was the only plan they had.

They found a sturdy tree at the edge of the crater that held Aeldbird. There, Elena untied the piece of rope she'd been using as a belt and looped one end around Victor's ankle. She threw the other end over a high branch, ran underneath, caught it, and tied it back on itself. Victor pulled on it lightly with his foot to test the knot. He wasn't convinced.

'Are you sure this is going to work?' said Victor.

'Nah,' said Elena. 'But it might.'

'What if I'm not high enough?'

'I'll pull you higher.'

'What if they come after you instead?'

'They're animals, not detectives. Just make sure you keep their attention. Wave and shout and whatever. Don't stop until I give you the signal.'

They got into their positions.

'Hello!' shouted Victor. 'I'm here and I'm delicious and I'm not on a roof!'

Noses swung in his direction.

Mouths watered.

As the animals raced out of the town, charging toward the trembling Victor, Elena ran into the cover of a bush and pulled on the rope as fiercely as she could manage. It launched Victor into the air.

He hung from the branch of the tree by his foot and felt all of the blood in his body pooling in his head.

Below him, the animals gnashed their teeth and swiped their claws through the air. The higher they reached, the higher Elena pulled Victor. He kept his eyes squeezed shut. He tried to picture his bed at home. He imagined his parents and the smallest mountain and playing cottleball on the village green.

Mingus leapt nimbly off the roof on which he'd been trapped, sprinting up out of the village and finding safety in the forest.

Soon the animals below Victor realised that they weren't going be having dinner any time soon. They slunk off to continue haunting the houses of the people who'd once hunted them. The villagers of Aeldbird didn't notice. They had their eyes pressed firmly into their stereoscopes, watching joyful people dance on beaches and spin each other in glittering ballrooms.

Elena lowered Victor to the ground. He picked himself up and brushed himself off.

'That wasn't so bad, was it?' she asked.

'You weren't hanging over a vicious bunch of hungry bears.'

'You're exaggerating.'

He stuck out his tongue.

She stuck out her tongue too.

They found Mingus sitting cross-legged beside the path. When he saw them, he jumped up and dragged them both into a hug. Elena pushed him away. Victor found himself unexpectedly grateful for the physical contact, even if it was slightly sweaty.

'Thank you, thank you,' Mingus said. 'I thought I was bear food for sure. But you saved me!'

'You're welcome,' said Victor.

'Any time,' said Elena.

'Now, what's the plan? I can't go back there. I'll either get eaten or have to watch everyone else get eaten.'

'We're going to find that man,' said Elena. 'Walter Swizwit. So he can fix everything. And you're going to help us, since we saved you. Do you know where he went?'

Mingus nodded eagerly.

'Then let's go!' said Elena, leaping to her feet.

'But it's getting dark,' said Victor. 'Shouldn't we stop?'

'And eat?' asked Mingus hopefully. 'Mum says I get silly when I'm hungry which just means I'll start annoying you and I don't want to annoy you because you seem nice and you saved me.'

They lit a fire, cooked a handful of pearl barley that Mingus kept in a pouch at his waist, and drank cups of lavender tea as the sun dissolved behind the trees.

'So everyone in your village hunts animals?' asked Victor.

With his mouth full, Mingus nodded. 'We chase them and catch them in nets and cages and then we keep them until the collectors come and take them away. Once a month, the collectors turn up. I hate them. When they get here, I hide in the cupboard under the sink. The collectors give me hot ears which sounds funny but it's actually pretty painful.' Mingus burped. 'If I'm honest, I hide a lot. My grandad said there are more things to be brave at than hunting animals, but as long as the collectors keeping coming to Aeldbird, hunting's all that counts.'

'Do the collectors own everything in your town too?' said Victor.

'Oh yes,' said Mingus. 'They gave us our houses and we have to pay them back. Everything is theirs and they bring us clothes and nets and fish and all the things we need.'

'Why don't you make your own clothes?'

Elena rolled her eyes.

Mingus stopped chewing. 'Is that possible?' he said. 'You can make your own clothes?'

'Of course it's possible,' said Victor.

'How do you do it?'

'Well, first you shave the sheep.'

'You shave the sheep?' said Mingus, shocked. 'Don't the sheep get cold?'

'I don't think so,' said Victor. 'Not if you make sure to shave them in the summer.'

'Then what do you do to the sheep?'

Victor laughed. 'You don't do anything to the sheep. You take the wool you shaved off and spin it into long thin bits.'

'Right,' said Mingus. 'Long thin bits.'

'And then you sort of just make them into clothes.'

'But how exactly do you make them into clothes?'

Victor struggled to come up with an answer. 'You kind of . . . tie them together.'

Mingus looked down at the tunic he was wearing. It didn't look like long thin bits tied together. 'Do you really?'

he said. 'I would never have guessed that.'

'Don't listen to him,' said Elena. 'He told me if you put bits of food in the ground, then more food comes out.'

'It's true!'

'I'm not sure I want to put my food into the ground,' said Mingus. 'I think I'm just going to eat mine, if that's okay.'

Victor sighed and gave up.

Once it was dark and everyone had settled down to sleep, Mingus appeared at the entrance to Victor's tent.

'Pssst,' he whispered. 'Can I have the tortoise?'

Victor blinked, half-asleep. 'What for?' he asked.

'I'm scared.'

'The tortoise won't protect you from anything.'

'I know, I just don't want to be alone and I'm cold and I keep thinking ghosts are going to come into my tent.'

'Mingus, I don't mean to be rude, but is there anything you're not afraid of?'

Mingus smiled. 'My dad said he was sure there must be a beast I wasn't afraid of, but that you'd have to walk to the end of the earth to find it.' He paused. 'So could I please have the tortoise with me, please?'

Victor nodded at Saint Oswald and watched him waddle out to Mingus's tent, where the boy wrapped the tortoise in his arms and fell into a dream hectic with balloons.

10

Saint Oswald awoke in the arms of an unfamiliar boy. He struggled to free himself. The more he wriggled, the closer the boy held him.

'*Uk, uk,*' said Saint Oswald.

Finally, Victor emerged from his own tent and discovered what was going on. He stood over the giant tortoise, laughing a little, but also apologising.

He nudged Mingus to try and wake him up.

'Hey,' Victor whispered. 'It's time to get up. I think you might be making my tortoise a little uncomfortable.'

'*Uk, uk,*' said Saint Oswald.

Still, Mingus slept on.

Unlike Elena, who had appeared at his side and knew exactly what to do.

'Here,' she said. 'I'll wake him up.'

Without warning, she emptied a flask of water into a bowl

and emptied the bowl over Mingus's face.

He spluttered awake with a scream, arms in the air.

'Argh!' he roared.

It took several deep breaths and long wails until he'd calmed down.

'What did you do that for? I thought I was drowning.'

'You weren't waking up,' said Elena. 'And you were about to squeeze that turtle to death. We need to get going.'

There was only time for a quick breakfast of sugarsnap peas and pigeon eggs. After that, they took down the tents, washed up the dishes and packed everything on to the cart.

Both Victor and Elena admitted that they had no idea where they ought to go next.

'I think I know,' said Mingus. 'The inventor asked people if they knew any villages richer than ours. Someone told him about a place called Sektun-Layley, pointed in that direction, and that was where he went.'

So that was the way they went too.

The woods that lay ahead of them bore little resemblance to what had come before. More and more of the sky began to show through the canopy. A ceiling of endless blue replaced the old stained-glass green. It was as though they were walking forward through the year, out of autumn and into winter. No one mentioned it. Perhaps, they were thinking, if we don't mention it, it will stop.

'Are we almost there?' Elena asked.

'I'm not sure,' said Mingus. 'I've never been *there* before, I've only ever been *here*.'

Soon, none of the trees wore any leaves. The temperature dropped too. Victor dug out an old jumper for Mingus and wrapped himself in some of the fabric they usually used for tents. Elena turned to skipping to warm herself up. She'd skip on ahead then loop back around them, lifting her legs high to keep the blood circulating.

'I think I can see something,' she said.

Sektun-Layley did not look like any village Victor had ever heard of. Each of its buildings was different to those surrounding it. They were all made of intricate combinations of brick, metal, plastic and glass. Some rose clumsily toward the sky; others lay long and low to the ground. There were pyramid-shaped buildings made entirely of glass. There were buildings covered in long poles of thin metal so that they looked like metal spiders. Between the houses, perfect paths of white stone led from door to door. Downsized replicas of trees lined the paths. Those trees, at least, still had their leaves.

The village, like the villages before it, was deserted.

The only sign of life was a small girl sitting cross-legged

outside one of the houses. The girl was untangling a tangle of copper wire. She was dressed all in white, with socks pulled up to her knees and hair tied scruffily into a bun.

'Hi,' the girl said, as they entered the village. She didn't seem surprised or afraid, and only looked up from the wire when she noticed Saint Oswald. 'I like your tortoise.'

'He's actually a turtle,' said Elena.

'He actually isn't,' said Victor.

'Turtles are aquatic,' said the girl. 'Tortoises are semi-aquatic. You can tell them apart by whether they have flippers or legs. It's simple really. Unless they have tessellating patterns on their shells, then—' The girl cut herself off by pulling on her hair. 'Stop it,' she said to herself.

Saint Oswald raised a leg as if to prove what he was.

'I told you,' said Victor to Elena.

'What kind of village is this?' asked Mingus. 'Is it from the future? I've always wanted to visit the future. I've heard very good things about it. Apparently, in the future, people can fly by flapping their legs. Is that true?'

'No,' the girl said. 'It's not. This is a research outpost. Sektun-Layley, named after its founders.'

With a swift, sharp movement, Elena pulled the bow from her back, fitted an arrow to the string and aimed it at the sitting girl.

'Tell us everything you know right now,' she demanded.

'Elena!' said Victor. 'Put that down. You can't say you're going to shoot everyone.'

The girl holding the ball of wire didn't look at all worried. 'Are you really planning to shoot me with an arrow?'

'No,' said Victor. 'She's not.'

'I might be,' said Elena. 'What if she's a collector? Or the inventor in disguise?'

'A collector is never without his cloak,' said the girl. 'And if you're talking about the same inventor that passed through here then he's significantly larger and more lumpy than I am.'

Elena lowered her bow. 'You saw him too?'

'From up on the roof. That's where I was when everything changed. That man arrived in our village and now everyone is stuck inside their houses, refusing to come out.'

'Did he wear a handkerchief around his neck?'

'And drive a broken old wagon?'

'And say that he was from the Deepest East?'

'Yes,' said the girl. 'It was the same man; he said his name was Walter Swizwit. He sold everyone these rather inaccurate tiny farms and now all they do is sit inside and play with them. They move pretend pigs around pretend barns and refuse to do any real work. At first, they would giggle to themselves as they did it, now they all do it as seriously as they ever did real work. I have no idea what's gotten into them. And I've tried everything to get them away. Did the same thing happen to all of you?'

'Sort of,' said Victor.

They told their stories, one by one.

'*Uk, uk,*' said Saint Oswald, in conclusion.

'That's terrible,' said the girl. She clearly didn't want to dwell on it.

'What do you do here?' asked Elena, trying to make up for having been so hasty.

'Whatever they ask us to do.'

'The collectors?'

The girl nodded. 'Every month they come and give us a new task, like creating a flower that never stops blooming or a dog that can't bark. Then they come again, take away whatever we've created, and give us food and clothes and test tubes for more experiments. We owe them a lot, so we have to pay them back.'

'But couldn't you work out how to make your own food and clothes and test tubes?'

'Make our own test tubes?' asked the girl. 'Out of glass?'

'Yes,' said Victor. 'All you need to do is make sand really, really hot.'

'Not again,' sighed Elena.

The girl nodded. 'That sounds highly unlikely to me.'

'It's true!'

'Perhaps it is.' She cleared her throat. 'Anyway, what are your names?'

They told her.

'I'm Mo-Lan,' the girl said. 'Do you want to see something amazing?'

They all agreed they did.

The girl led them into a long, silver building, with a roof made of glass. Inside, the building was perfectly clean. There was not a single smudge of dirt on any of the walls. Out of curiosity, Victor pressed his thumb against it. His grubby fingerprint flickered for a second and then disappeared entirely. He gasped.

'This way,' called Mo-Lan.

She led them along a long, wide corridor. Hundreds of doors of different shapes and sizes led off it. None of them were labelled but Mo-Lan seemed to know exactly where she was going.

Eventually she ushered them into a room that smelled of hay and toffee.

The children stood in front of three beasts the size of tractors. The creatures were almost perfectly round, covered in shaggy red hair, and watched the world through big eyes that shone as though their owners had just received heart-breaking news.

'These are ogoropods,' Mo-Lan explained. 'The middle one's Miss Buttons, the other two are Pablo and Jonty. Miss Buttons is my favourite, even though you're not supposed to have favourites. We have the same birthday.'

The children took them in. The creatures were bigger than anything they'd ever seen. They let out moos so deep and loud that you could feel the vibrations through the soles of your feet. Each ogoropod had nine udders hanging from its belly.

'They look like cows,' said Victor.

'But fatter.'

'In a way, they are. They are cows that have been changed to produce as much milk as possible. Instead of making milk in their udders, they make it in their bellies. They get bigger and bigger until the milk is drained out of them.'

'Doesn't that hurt?'

'I suppose it must do. They were trying to make more milk, not happier cows. Miss Buttons always seems like she's in pain, though – that's why I come and read to her. She likes poems best, ones that rhyme. For me, poems are always—'

Once again, Mo-Lan pulled on her hair to stop herself talking.

'Why do you keep doing that?' asked Mingus. 'It looks painful.'

'Sometimes I think too much,' said Mo-Lan. 'They teach us to think all the time because if we're not thinking, then we're wasting valuable seconds. We have to think constantly to come up with new things for the collectors, but sometimes I think too much about the wrong things and when that happens I pull on my hair and it lets my brain know it has to stop.'

She blinked.

'Sometimes I think too much too,' said Mingus. 'But mostly about what I'm going to eat or what's going to eat me.'

Mo-Lan smiled. 'Do you want to see something else?' she said.

Four doors down, they stepped into a room with a ceiling as high as a cathedral. It needed to be that high as the turnip that occupied the room was the size of a comfortable three-bedroomed house. It reminded Victor of a planet. It was bulging and bumpy and the colour of a two-day-old bruise.

'This is the giant turnip,' explained Mo-Lan. 'It never stops growing. Every morning, it has to have pieces cut off it. People go up on ladders and shave pieces off the side.'

'Otherwise what?'

'Otherwise it would keep growing until it knocked the moon out of the sky. Anyway, it means we have to have turnip for breakfast every single morning so I wouldn't say it was the best invention in the world.'

'And the collectors ask you to make all of this?' asked Elena.

'Yes,' said the girl, looking at her feet. 'They give us all the laboratory equipment and tools and resources to create everything, so they get to decide which things we create.' She lowered her voice. 'But there are secret projects too, ones that they don't know about. Do you want to see one? It's a little scary and we'll have to be careful, but it's remarkable too, and it's going to change the world. Come on.'

This time, they walked to the end of the corridor and came to a door marked with a black cross. It looked ominous.

Mo-Lan took a lantern from the floor and lit it with a match. She pushed open the heavy door, revealing a darkness that seemed as solid as brick.

'Be slow,' she said. 'And quiet. You don't want to spook him.'

One by one, they stepped inside.

Mingus screamed.

Victor placed himself firmly behind Elena.

And Elena's mouth fell open in amazement.

The creature they were staring at was a spider the size of a car. Its legs were as thick as a farmer's arms and its eyes were the size of tortoise shells. Great, cream-coloured fangs hung from its mandible, each one tipped with a protective piece of cork. The creature was posed behind a web of glittering threads that looked almost as though they'd been spun from glass.

'Is that real?' Elena said.

'Of course he's real,' said Mo-Lan. 'We call him Dr Katz.'

'Why?'

'Everyone's got to have a name, it's only fair. He spins web that's so strong, you'd need an axe to cut through it. It could be used for all kinds of things, and it's sustainable, and you can harvest as much of it as you want.'

Elena had a question. 'You know what you're doing,' she said. 'So why do you need the others? Can't you look after all the animals yourself?'

Mo-Lan shook her head. 'I don't know how to do any of the things properly. I can't milk the ogoropods without hurting them. I can't cut the turnip without killing it. And I don't know how to get the cobwebs away from the spider without it attacking me. If something doesn't change, everything we've worked to create will be in trouble and the collectors will come for our village. They own everything.

They'll leave us with nothing at all.'

'You could come with us?' said Victor. 'We're going to find the inventor and make him come back to fix everything. Only we're not sure where he went.'

'He said he was going to Kaftan Minor,' said Mo-Lan. 'Which is around two days' walk from where we're standing.'

Mo-Lan thought for a second. 'I'll come,' she said. 'But we'll have to be as quick as possible. I don't know how long our village will survive without help. If we're not there to control them, the experiments will run wildly out of control. It could be possible that the turnip expands beyond all control or Dr Katz gets free or—' She pulled on her hair.

They waited as she packed a bag, said goodbye to the animals of Sektun-Layley, and dabbed a few tears off her cheeks.

'You okay?' asked Victor.

'I suppose I'll have to be,' said Mo-Lan.

Victor had never had so much company before. He wasn't quite sure how to behave. It was enough to have to worry about what one other person was thinking or feeling or planning or wanting to eat and now there were three other people and he had no idea what was going on in any of their heads.

'*Uk, uk,*' said Saint Oswald.

'Sorry,' said Victor. 'Four other people.'

A few steps ahead of him, Mo-Lan leaned over to Mingus and whispered, 'Did he just talk to his tortoise?'

'He does that sometimes,' said Mingus. 'And be careful if you're ever having a nice and peaceful dream because then the other one might throw a bucket of water over you and wake you up and act like it was your fault completely.'

Together, the five of them carried on along the path that wound through the woods. None of the children knew what would come next. They did not know where the path would take them, whether they would ever find the inventor, or what would happen if they did.

11

The four children and the speedy tortoise made their way carefully through the outer edge of the forest.

'Can I ask you all something?' said Victor.

'As long as it's not about seeds or sheep or glass,' said Elena.

'It's not. But I was wondering, what happens if you just stop giving the collectors what they want? What if you stopped giving them rubies and animals and whatever else they ask for? What if you run out or get sick?'

'If you don't give them what they want,' said Elena, 'they take you away. It happened to my aunt. She started getting these headaches which meant she couldn't see properly to mine rubies. When the collectors came they took her because she didn't have enough to give them.' Elena looked close to tears. 'My uncle went after them to try to get her back but no one ever saw him again either.'

Victor was horrified. 'Where did they take them?'

'Nobody knows,' says Mingus. 'But I heard it's a huge dark castle that even the sun is too scared to go inside and they make you work until you can't any more and then they throw you into a bottomless pit.'

Victor's mouth fell open. 'But why?' he said. 'How can they do that?'

'Our villages owe them,' said Mo-Lan. 'For the houses and the tools and everything else. We are in their debt. That's why we have to do what they tell us.'

'But surely you've paid them back by now,' said Victor, looking at Mingus. 'You said you've been hunting animals since your great-great-grandfather.'

Mingus nodded. 'But every year we owe them more.'

'That's not fair!' shouted Victor. 'Why?'

'Because they bring us food and clothes,' said Elena.

'I told you already, you can make those things!'

'Yes,' she said. 'But even if we knew how, we couldn't, because we have to collect the rubies to pay them back.'

Victor fell silent. It hurt his head to think about the situation his three companions were in. They had to work to pay for food that they couldn't grow because they were too busy working. What kind of sense did that make? He wished they could see Rainwater, with its fields of golden wheat and plump vegetables and trees dotted with apples waiting to be cooked into great jars of sticky jam.

After walking for a few hours, they came across a clearing in the woods where a towering, yellow stone stood. The stone was as tall as a house and shaped like a crumbling hunk of cheese. Green beards of pale moss hung from its extremities and tiny flowers peeped out of its cracks and the whole thing cast a long, dark shadow across the ground.

'What's that supposed to be?' asked Elena, putting her hands on her hips and angling her head as though the stone might make more sense when looked at horizontally.

'It looks scary,' said Mingus.

'That's the Rock of Little Regard,' said Mo-Lan. 'I've seen it on a map once. People say it's haunted but my parents don't believe in ghosts. Mum says only guilty people see ghosts and that they're the conscience climbing out of the head to make sure you don't forget the things you've done wrong.'

'Then we should sleep in there,' said Elena, taking a few steps forward. 'If people think it's haunted, no one's going to sneak in at night.'

'But the ghosts,' said Mingus. 'What if the ghosts come in?'

Elena sighed. 'Didn't you listen? She said there aren't ghosts.'

'That's not strictly true,' explained Mo-Lan. 'I said there aren't ghosts as we commonly understand them. There are in fact ghosts for the—' She stopped speaking when Elena gave her hair a gentle tug.

'You can't pull her hair!' said Mingus.

'It's okay,' said Mo-Lan, looking slightly annoyed nonetheless. 'I probably needed to stop thinking.'

'Shall we go in?' suggested Victor, who wanted more than anything to avoid an argument. 'Maybe the inventor used it as a camp too, and he left a clue. Maybe he's even still there.'

In single file, with Mingus at the back, they trooped into the Rock of Little Regard. Inside, there was just enough light to illuminate the ground they were walking on. The four children held hands.

'I don't think we should go any further,' said Mingus.

'There's definitely no inventor in here,' said Elena.

'I'll light a fire,' promised Victor, who could see that Mingus didn't feel particularly comfortable in the gloom. He crouched and built a pyramid from the handful of sticks he'd taken with him from the cart. Then, using his flint and a harkstone, he began scratching sparks out of the dark air.

Once the bundle of twigs leapt into flames, Mo-Lan gasped.

They were surrounded.

All around them stood creatures and men, from fierce bears to hunched old women, petrified badgers to crying giants. None of the animals, human or otherwise, were moving. Each was made entirely of ancient metal, covered with a thick layer of crumbling rust. Many of them had lost fingers, claws, toes and noses. Almost all of the iron statues looked afraid.

'What are they?' asked Elena.

While Mo-Lan eyed the metal figures curiously, Mingus had fallen to the floor and curled up in a ball with his eyes closed. Elena whipped her bow out and aimed an arrow at the metal head of a sad-looking woman dressed in a ragged skirt.

Victor, who was still blowing at the flames, hadn't noticed anything. He'd assumed the others had gasped because he'd managed to start a fire and he'd felt quietly proud of himself. It wasn't until Saint Oswald started nipping at the hem of his trousers that he looked up.

'I know what these are!' he said. 'The Great Aunt told me. These are creatures from the Iron Plague.'

'Creatures?' whispered a fear-struck Mingus, from his ball.

'It's okay,' said Mo-Lan, patting him. 'You can open your eyes. They're not alive.'

Hesitantly, Mingus let one eye fall open. The fact that none of the men or beasts around them were moving did very little to calm his nerves. 'I thought the Iron Plague was a myth,' he mumbled.

'It was real,' said Elena. 'But it happened ten billion years ago.' She looked at Mo-Lan as though daring her to challenge the number. Mo-Lan decided against it. 'What happened was an evil wizard cast a spell that made everyone turn slowly into metal. Once none of them could move any more, he got the clouds to start pouring out this horrible rain that melted them all. Eventually, almost everyone was gone. But these people must have hidden here, which meant they turned to iron but never got melted away.'

'But why would anyone want to do that?' asked Victor.

'Because he was an evil wizard,' said Elena, like it was the most obvious thing in the world.

'There's no such thing as an evil wizard,' said Mo-Lan. 'The idea of magic goes completely against the fundamentals of physics.'

'Well maybe the fungermentals were different back then,' said Elena, sticking out her tongue. 'You wouldn't know. You weren't there.'

Mo-Lan rolled her eyes. 'And you weren't at Blackwater when King Marshalla defeated the Sorry Army but I'm sure you believe it was an event that occurred.'

'That's different.'

'In what way?'

'It just is.'

The children fell silent and sat warming themselves by the fire. Without noticing it, they had all moved as close to the flames as possible once they'd glimpsed the creatures surrounding them. There was something about them that filled Victor with dread. That, together with the argument between Mo-Lan and Elena, made him feel restless and upset. This was not the kind of problem he'd ever had to deal with before. It was impossible to fall out with Saint Oswald. He'd accidentally stood on him once while getting out of bed but Victor had just brought him an extra couple of river cucumbers for breakfast and all had been forgiven.

Victor had an idea.

Without explaining himself, he scuttled out of the giant rock and dashed around the woods collecting ferns and flowers and shreds of bark as the last of the daylight slipped from the sky. Back inside the rock, he brewed them in a pot over the fire.

Once they had warm cups in their hands and warm tea in their bellies, the children quickly forgot that they'd been arguing at all. There was something special about the tea and it filled them up almost as much as a good meal. Victor realised something then: it can be very easy to confuse hunger with anger.

'Do you think we'll be in a city soon?' he asked.

'By my calculations, we'll arrive tomorrow afternoon,' said Mo-Lan.

'And there will be lots of people?'

'Trillions,' said Elena.

'Storytellers and musicians and actors?'

'And scientists and vets and dentists and accountants,' said Mo-Lan.

'I hope they like us,' said Mingus. 'And I hope they don't make us hunt anything.'

'If they do,' said Elena, 'I'll shoot them with my bow.'

Mingus smiled. 'That's nice of you.'

By the flickering light of the fire, watched over by a menagerie of iron animals, the children dropped off to sleep.

12

'**G**oodbye metal people,' whispered Mingus as they left the next morning.

Gradually, the track became a path and the path became a road. Trees grew further and further apart. Rather than forcing a way on to the path, the overgrowth stayed respectfully at its border.

And people began to pass them.

First, a scrap-metal merchant, with a cow-drawn cart.

Next, a botanist carrying a glass case filled with strange plants.

Victor, who'd been beginning to doubt that they'd ever leave the forest, was growing excited. Soon enough, they'd be in a city. An actual city, with tearooms and ballrooms and a thousand other kinds of rooms. And there would be people, more people than he could count, doing things he'd never even imagined.

It was late afternoon when the spires of the city came into view. They all paused to take it in, watching in amazement as the sun began to dip below the jumble of buildings. The city spread like a patchwork quilt across the land and climbed high into the mountains that rose behind it. Its buildings were packed together along the winding streets, paved with wonky cobbles and coloured with wild weeds and stubborn flowers. There were grand spires and stone towers and ancient statues all reaching toward the pink clouds.

A river curled through the centre of Kaftan Minor. Buildings leant over the water like fishermen and lamp posts gazed at their own glowing orange reflections as the sun slipped away behind the snow-dusted hills. At the far end of the city, on a hill between the mountains and the crowded streets, stood a crooked castle built from grey stone. Ragged banners hung from its battlements, though they were too distant for the children to read.

'It's so big,' said Victor, in amazement. He could barely imagine how much must be going on in such a vast place. How many plans were being hatched and expeditions were being planned and dreams were being dreamt? Kaftan Minor, thought Victor, had to be the start and end of a thousand different adventures.

'Not very loud,' said Elena. 'Is it?'

'And I can smell it from here,' said Mingus. 'What's that smell?'

'Wee,' said Elena.

'Ammonia,' said Mo-Lan. 'And tar.'

They entered the city cautiously. It was quiet, but not a peaceful quiet, more of a secretive, clawing quiet, that lay ready to be broken. Though lights shone in windows, the only people in the streets were busy-looking folk with places to be. A few deliverymen dashed between doorways with great sacks loaded on to their bicycles. Lamplighters climbed spindly ladders to ignite the lanterns at the tops of the street lights.

Victor's heart sank. Was this really it? The great city from the stories brought from over the mountains? Parts of it may have looked grand, but the streets were virtually empty. It was barely livelier than any of their villages. Though there must have been thousands of people in the buildings, none of them seemed to want to come out. *Perhaps*, he thought, *there is a vicious beast that prowls the town at night, and everyone's too afraid to come out after dark. They must all be waiting for the creature to be slain before they can relax again.*

The four children and the giant tortoise passed dusty market stalls, boarded-up shops and abandoned furniture. Fat rats scurried up drainpipes and lazy pigeons pecked mushy crumbs from the gutters. The houses were falling apart, paint peeling and deep cracks climbing their walls like vines.

Warm orange glowed from the windows of a bar called The Dozy Pony. It was decided that a pub would be as good a place as any to ask after the inventor. Inside, there was no one but the bartender, sitting bored behind the bar, flicking through a book and occasionally grunting with annoyance.

The three children argued about who would ask the questions. No one really wanted to do it. As they bickered, the bartender's eyes lifted from the page she was reading to scrutinise her unexpected guests. To hurry things up, Elena volunteered. She marched up to the bar and dumped her fists directly on it.

'Hello,' she said, trying her best to sound older and more serious than she felt.

The bartender glanced over the top of her book.

'Can I help you?' she replied.

'We're looking for a man called Walter Swizwit,' explained Elena. 'He wears a handkerchief around his neck and sells pointless things to people who don't need them.'

The woman didn't seem surprised. 'After Walter, are you?'

'We are,' said Elena. 'Do you know where he is?'

'Of course I knows where he is, everyone in this city knows where he is. He bought the castle on the back hill not long ago. We hear all sorts of noise coming from that place now. Funny lights in the windows, explosions blowing off the roof every three days.'

'The castle?'

'Used to belong to some duke or another, a few hundred years ago. You don't see many dukes about these days though, eh? Been empty until Swizwit snapped it up. No one else could afford it, see? Made a nice stash of money from his inventions, he has.'

'Can I ask you something else?' said Elena.

'You can ask, I might not answer.'

Elena wasn't deterred. 'Why is the town so empty? I thought cities were supposed to be loud. Aren't there supposed to be busy markets and performers and people bustling about everywhere?'

The woman shrugged. 'Times change,' she said. 'People don't need to leave their houses now, so they don't.'

'They don't leave their houses?'

'Things come to them, they don't come to things. Anyhow, most of them are too in debt to those bleeding collectors to spend an evening drinking dandelion tea in here.' The bartender shook her head sadly. 'What can you do? There's no going back now.' She tutted. 'Now, are you going to order something, or can I get on with running my failing business?'

'That's it, thanks for your help.'

'My pleasure.'

She hurried back to share the new information with everyone else. They all fell into silent disappointment on learning that the city was no longer the kind of city they had once imagined. Victor especially felt saddened.

'At least we know where the inventor is,' said Mingus, which didn't do much to cheer anyone up.

In the dim light of Kaftan Minor's lamp posts, they headed for the crooked castle on the hill. With every step they took, Victor felt more and more despondent. The city was even deader than Rainwater. At least at home people left their houses to gossip and trade and work in the fields. Here, there were virtually no signs of life. It was as though they'd stumbled into a town that had been totally abandoned.

'Maybe it's not normally this bad,' said Elena, trying to raise Victor's spirits. 'Maybe they're preparing for an attack.'

Victor said nothing.

'Or they're scared of something,' said Mingus. 'Something really big and hungry.'

Victor said nothing.

'It might be the case that all of the inhabitants are simply occupied,' suggest Mo-Lan. 'They might be hiding away in their rooms in order to put together plans for altering their—'

She pulled on her hair and stopped talking.

Still, Victor said nothing.

13

The castle was a dark, grand building built of grey stone. It had been fitted with new windows and doors and decked out with tropical plants that hung like chandeliers from its battlements. The result was a building that straddled two time periods and looked like it belonged to neither.

A moat of murky water encircled the castle. Luckily, the drawbridge was lowered, though the door it led to was half a metre thick and criss-crossed with bands of iron. It looked impenetrable. From within the castle, the sound of clashing swords rung out.

It sounded like a vast army was training inside its walls.

'What do we do now?' whispered Mingus.

'We just knock, I suppose,' suggested Victor. 'And we try to explain what's happened. It can't hurt him to help us. Maybe the whole thing's a misunderstanding.'

'There's no way that'll work,' said Elena.

'From what we know of Walter Swizwit,' said Mo-Lan, 'it does seem incredibly unlikely that he'll fold to our demands.'

'Does anyone else have another idea?'

No one did.

They unhooked the supply cart from Saint Oswald and hid it around one corner of the castle. Hopefully, it would still be there when they left.

Elena rapped on the door.

It was five minutes before anyone answered.

A bald butler in a purple bow tie peered around the door at the children. He stood very rigid, with one hand folded across his belly and the other grasping the handle of the door. His nostrils flared as though he was being forced to smell rotten fruit.

'Yes?' he said, in a voice that sounded like a creaking hinge.

'We need to speak to Walter Swizwit,' said Victor. 'It's important.'

The man raised his eyebrows. 'I'm sorry,' he said. 'That's not possible.'

And he slammed the door with such force that Mingus fell backwards.

Mo-Lan helped him up.

'What do we do now?' said Elena.

Victor pointed to a large open window positioned high in the castle wall. 'We could try going that way.'

'I'm not sure that's a good idea,' said Mingus. 'What if we fall and break our legs or land in the moat and get eaten by hungry fishes?'

Mo-Lan raised her hand as though she was in a classroom and wanted to ask something from the teacher. 'If we do attempt it,' she said, 'there will be a certain probability that we fall and hurt ourselves. But if we don't try, there will be a one hundred per cent chance that our parents get taken away by the collectors.'

And so it was decided.

First, a trembling Mingus stood below the window and Mo-Lan climbed up on to his shoulders. Then Elena climbed up Mingus and up Mo-Lan and in through the window. Victor followed her up, then the two of them worked together to pull Mo-Lan, Mingus and Saint Oswald up.

'We did it,' said Mingus, breathing a sigh of relief. 'And we're alive.'

'Just about,' said Elena.

The children found themselves in an opulently decorated corridor. Dark oil paintings of stark landscapes hung from the walls and marble sculptures of exotic beasts stood on stone plinths. A narrow, lush red carpet ran along the floor. Torches burned in stone alcoves.

Through a door at one end of the corridor, someone was singing an old folk song in a hideous, screeching voice. The children recognised it at once as the voice of the man who had rolled into their villages in his carriage.

Elena ran to the door and threw it open.

Walter Swizwit was lying in a golden bathtub, covered in pearlescent bubbles. The bathroom in which the bathtub sat was also golden, as was the toilet and the sink and large, coin-shaped soap that lay between the taps.

At the sound of the children's footsteps, the inventor's eyes snapped open. His song ended mid-note and his face filled with shock. Half a second later, anger replaced the shock and the spindly man brought a fist crashing through his bathwater.

'Who are you?' he demanded to know. 'How did you get in here?'

'I'm from Rainwater,' said Victor, taking a step forward.

'And I'm from Moonwald,' said Elena.

'Aeldbird,' said Mingus.

'And Sektun-Layley,' said Mo-Lan.

'Do you think I give a broken goose where you're from?' said the inventor in the bath. 'Is that supposed to mean something to me? Give me one reason not to have my guards throw you off the highest tower.'

Mingus scuttled behind Mo-Lan.

Saint Oswald drew his head into his shell.

And Victor dug his fingernails into the heels of his hands. 'They're the names of our villages and we need you to tell us how to get our parents back. You poisoned mine and turned all of theirs into zombies that won't do anything apart from play with your stupid toys.'

The inventor chuckled to himself. 'Isn't that up to them? Are they not grown adults, perfectly capable of making their own decisions?'

'But they made terrible decisions!' said Elena. 'And it wasn't like they really knew what they were getting into.'

Walter Swizwit shook his head. 'That, my gap-toothed child, is the price of freedom. It's not freedom if you can't mess it up. Now put that bow down before I have someone come up here and shove it down your throat.'

Slowly, Elena lowered her bow.

'It's not freedom if you don't know what you're doing,' said Mo-Lan. 'It's not freedom if you've been misled.'

'What would you know about it? You can't be older than twelve. You've never worked a day in your life, never felt the burden of having to make enough money to feed yourself or keep a roof over your head.'

'We help in our villages,' said Mingus. 'And we know how horrible it is when the collectors come, asking for more when we don't have more.'

The inventor laughed, a deep, sad, horrible laugh. 'Those lot still saddling you faraway-folk with debt?'

'They were,' said Elena. 'But now everyone's so obsessed with your pointless toys that they're not doing any work and the next time the collectors come, they'll have nothing to collect.'

'I'm sure they'll still find a way of taking back what they're owed. Again, your parents chose to borrow from those brutes; they can't be surprised when repayment is requested.'

'Our parents were tricked,' said Elena. 'By the collectors and by you.'

That was more than enough for Walter Swizwit. 'Enough,' he said. 'I am bored of this conversation.' He put his fingers in his mouth and blew a swift, piercing whistle that cut through the air like an arrow. 'You have disturbed what is only my third bath of the day, left muddy footprints all the way down my ninth favourite corridor, and are now standing around spouting nonsense while I'm working very hard at trying to relax. It really is appalling behaviour. I had hoped you might've been sent to order further batches of my inventions for your pokey little hamlets, but you've come to blame me for the idiocy of your own guardians.'

Three tall, broad, gruff men appeared in the doorway. They were dressed in uncomfortable-looking uniforms consisting of plates of metal and frilly puffs of lace. All of them were red-faced and panting with the effort of having to sprint madly across an entire castle.

Elena stepped forward before they could take hold of her.

'This is what you tricked our parents for?' she shouted at Walter Swizwit. 'Some bubbly water and a dressing gown? Is this really worth ruining all our lives for?'

'We have baths too,' said Mingus, more to himself than to anyone else. 'I don't like them because the water gets stuck in my earholes but Mum makes me have them anyway, just ours is wooden but I expect the water feels the same.'

'Water is only ever two parts hydrogen and one part oxygen,' said Mo-Lan. 'There's no way it can feel like anything else.'

For a moment, Walter Swizwit's face softened. The fire and the fury left it. He sank low in his bubble bath and gazed at the ceiling with glazed eyes. He was remembering his own childhood. How his mother would fill an old wine barrel with water they'd made warm over the fire and she'd make him and his sister take it in turns to step inside while she brushed them violently with a sponge tied to a stick. They'd always complain and wriggle but they enjoyed it really. On cold days, standing in the barrel would warm them up. And on hot days, they'd use freezing water from the stream and it would cool them both down.

Walter Swizwit sighed. How he wished he could climb back through time and be a child again.

'Who's this?' said Victor, turning around with a picture frame he'd picked up from the windowsill. The photograph in the frame showed a girl around the age of eight or nine. She had dirt smeared across her cheeks and was standing in front of a lopsided wood-beamed house.

Something about the picture sent the inventor's anger rushing back.

'You put that down!' shouted Walter Swizwit. 'Guards! Take them away!'

They marched forward to seize the children. Elena threw all of her weight against one of them and knocked him to the floor.

'Quick!' she shouted to the others.

But it was too late.

Mingus had already fallen to the ground and curled up into a ball with his eyes closed.

Mo-Lan was pulling on her hair, eyes darting around the room.

Only Victor put up any kind of fight, and he was so tired and hungry that he barely had the energy to push at the gleaming armour of the castle guards.

Seeing that the battle was lost, Elena gave herself up. She angrily shoved her hands out ahead of her so that they could be tied together with thick rope.

'Take them to the dungeon,' said the inventor. 'They will stay there until I think of something better for them to do.'

He clapped his hands.

The children and the tortoise were led away.

14

'You're all useless,' said Elena, in the gloom.

Victor rolled his eyes. 'There was no way we could have gotten away.'

'*Uk, uk,*' said Saint Oswald.

The dungeon was a damp stone room without any windows, where droplets of sour-smelling water fell from the ceiling. The only light came from a flickering torch on the distant wall. Heavy metal bars kept them from escaping.

Broken objects were strewn across the floor of the cell. There were shards of glass, lengths of string, strange dials and meters and cogs and switches. The objects seemed to be the remains of experiments gone wrong.

In one corner, old books were piled up, their pages wavy with wet air. In another, stained rags sat in a heap as tall as a person. As the children took in their surroundings, the torch on the wall went out, plunging them into a grey gloom.

'I just don't see how you could both do nothing,' said Elena, standing over Mingus and Mo-Lan.

'I was scared,' said Mingus, who was verging on tears.

'And I was trying to come up with a plan,' said Mo-Lan.

Elena threw her hands into the air. 'We had a plan! It was to fight if someone came to take us! Not to stand around like a bunch of idiots waiting to be captured!'

'But we don't know how to fight,' said Mo-Lan, getting to her feet and looking Elena square in the eye. 'It's not something we've ever done. And raising your voice at me and Mingus is highly unlikely to change the situation we've currently found ourselves in. Wouldn't you rather turn your mind to how we might get out, rather than how we got in?'

Elena shook her head with anger. 'Nah,' she said. 'We wouldn't be here if you two hadn't been so useless.'

'But we are here!' said Mingus. 'We're here and it's freezing and they probably won't bring us blankets because we're their enemies and I get gassy when I'm cold and my head hurts.'

For a while, they sat in silence, teeth chattering and knees knocking. Each child thought of home the way home had been before the inventor had passed through. They remembered pollen-heavy summer afternoons and winter nights by smoky fires and meals so big that after eating them, you fell straight asleep. They remembered being halfway up trees and halfway across rivers. They remembered bedtime stories told by exhausted parents.

'It's too quiet!' Mingus bellowed. 'I'm sick of being stuck in my head. Can someone say something?'

'Like what?' said Victor.

'Your tortoise, Saint Oswald, where did you get him? I've never seen a tortoise that big. There must be some kind of story to how you found him.'

Victor hesitated. He didn't feel much like talking. He wanted to lie down, sleep and dream that he was a million miles away. 'I don't know,' he said. 'I don't really feel like it.'

'Go on,' said Elena. 'A story wouldn't hurt. It might take our minds off this hole.'

'All right,' said Victor. 'I'll try, but I'm shivering.'

'Let's sit in a circle,' suggested Mo-Lan. 'That way we'll share body heat and keep each other warm with our breath.'

Grudgingly, they tried to arrange themselves in a circle, though Elena sat as far from Mo-Lan as possible, Mingus sat as far from Elena as he could, and Victor attempted to sit square in the middle of everyone else, so that they ended up in a wonky triangle instead.

Victor began his story.

'One night,' he said, 'a few summers ago, a travelling

trader came into our town from over the mountains. He had all kinds of things with him but he also had animals. There were bugs and guinea pigs and birds that could speak. There was Saint Oswald too, but he was only about the size of my hand then. The man was keeping him in a little metal cage that hung from the caravan and he was being bounced around every time the caravan went over a bump. Every time he made a sound in pain, the trader would whack the cage until he stopped.

'I watched him doing that all the way into town, from the mountain where I go every morning. Straight away, I ran home and made my dad promise to try and get the tortoise for me. That night, he went out to find the trader, who was drinking in our inn, and offered him a few coins for Saint Oswald.

'"I'm not selling him to you for that," the man said. "He's one of a kind. There's no other tortoise like that this side of the Eastern Ocean. He'll grow to be the size of a lion. He's worth more than this entire village put together."

'So my dad came back and told me it was impossible. I think I started crying. I told him all about how I'd seen the tortoise making *uk*, *uk* sounds and the trader smacking his cage until he went quiet. I told him we had to do something otherwise he could end up dead.

'My dad had an idea.

'He took a special kind of tea down from the back of the shelf, I think it was valerian mixed with something else, and he went back to the trader in the inn. He asked if he could see the tortoise. The trader didn't want to let him at first, but then my dad showed him this family heirloom we have, an ancient golden tiara, and said he would give that up along with our entire farm and all its animals in return for the tortoise.

'"I want to hold him first," my dad said. "I want to check he's healthy."

'So the trader gave over the tortoise and my dad snuck a pinch of the tea into its mouth. He turned him over a few times then handed him back, saying he wasn't right.

A few seconds later, the tortoise's eyes closed and his legs went floppy. The trader picked him up and shook him. And shook him harder. And shook him again. Nothing happened. He became furious.

'"What have you done to my tortoise?" he started shouting at my dad. "You've killed him! You killed my tortoise! He'll never grow now!" He was so angry, he flung Saint Oswald onto the floor.

'The man tried to attack my dad but everyone in the village was on his side. They'd seen how he treated his animals and wanted him gone as soon as possible. So everyone waved goodbye to the trader and made sure he left town. Dad scooped up Saint Oswald from the ground and brought him home to me. We put him in a bath of warm water then made a nest for him out of old towels. An hour or two later, he woke back up, and we've had him ever since.'

'*Uk, uk,*' said Saint Oswald.

Just as Victor finished speaking, a strange voice cut through the darkness.

'May I have a look?' it said.

15

The voice came from the pile of rags in the corner. They stirred and shook until a woman emerged. She was not much more than a skeleton, covered with paper-white skin and topped with a straggly mess of ginger hair. The hollows of her cheeks looked like pawprints in the snow. She raised a wiry finger and aimed it at Saint Oswald.

Terrified, the children threw themselves against the back wall.

Mingus put his hands over his eyes.

And Elena raised a fist either side of her head.

'Don't be afraid,' said the woman. 'There are far worse creatures in this castle than me, and I don't want to hurt you, I only want to examine the tortoise.'

'Who are you?' asked Victor.

'You won't know my name,' said the woman.

'Why did he put you down here?' Elena wanted to know.

The woman smiled sadly. 'So that the world doesn't find out.'

'Find out what?'

'That he stole my inventions and hid me here so that I wouldn't have the chance to tell the world what he'd done. I don't know what he's used them for but judging by the castle in which we find ourselves, it seems to be going rather well. He's a rich man now.'

'Why does he want to be so rich?' asked Mingus. 'It can't be that fun.'

'I have no idea,' said the thin woman. 'As far as I can tell, it doesn't make him happy. I suppose he wants what anyone with a little bit of money and power wants: a little more money and power. I heard once that he was raising an army, though all I hear him do now is sing and make things explode.'

'An army? For what?'

The thin woman shrugged. 'That, I couldn't tell you. This corner of the world hasn't seen war in a long time. To tell you my truth, I don't know Walter all that well. We met some time ago, in a steamer crossing the ocean back from the Old West. I had travelled there to try to sell three of my most important inventions, inventions that no one here would pay any attention to, but I had hoped others might see the value of. It was not to be. Once I arrived, I was told that in the Old West, it is illegal to invent anything new.'

'Illegal?' said Victor. 'Why would they make it illegal to invent things?'

'Because a long, long time ago, someone accidentally created something so powerful and terrible that it had the power to ruin many lives.'

'What was it?'

'To look at, it was nothing more than a simple music box. But if the stories are to be believed, the song it played was so powerful that all who heard it were doomed.' The woman shuddered at the thought of it. 'Anyway,' she continued. 'When I met Walter on that ship, he was returning home after a failed trip to try and make his fortune.

'I showed him the prototypes I had in my suitcase, thinking that he seemed like a curious type of person, and he was. He asked any number of questions about my creations. In all honesty, I was flattered, and more than happy to explain the basics of them to him.

'When I woke up the next morning, swinging in my hammock with the motion of the waves, my suitcase had vanished. It didn't take me long to realise Walter had taken it. But the ship docked before I could find him. I followed his trail of course, but by the time I'd found him, he'd already gained considerable resources. He soon had me captured and locked away. I've been his prisoner ever since. These past months have been desperately lonely, I'll tell you that, and I've spent every second regretting ever making those wretched machines. I have no idea what he's up to, no idea what he's doing, has done, or will do. In fact, I haven't seen him even once since he put me here.'

'What were your inventions?' asked Mo-Lan.

'Well,' said the woman. 'There was a kind of mirror that you could use to start a fire using only the sun, and a stereoscope that could show news from one side of the land to the other, and a small replica of a farm that could be used to teach children the basics of farming before they were ready to work in the fields.'

The children's mouths fell open.

'He's been selling them as his own inventions!' said Elena. 'They've turned our parents into zombies! When he gave mine the mirror, none of them could stop looking at themselves. Now all they care about is their own faces.'

'And all mine care about is looking through the weird goggles at people having a nicer time than them,' said Mingus.

'And mine only want to play with the tiny farms,' said Mo-Lan.

Distraught, the woman sank into herself like a popped balloon. 'I'm sorry to hear it,' she said. 'I truly am. It was never my intention to have those items used in such a way; they were only ever supposed to be released with careful instructions for their use. If I'd realised the damage they could have caused, I never would have brought them with me over the ocean.' She shook her head sadly. 'But the people of your kingdom don't live like they do in ours. Their time belongs to others, those that bought them long ago.'

'The collectors?' asked Victor.

'Yes. The trouble is, when your time belongs to others, you stop being able to value it, and you end up throwing it all away.'

'Would you be able to help us?' said Elena. 'If we ever got out of here, would you know how to turn our parents back to normal?'

'Of course – I am not so reckless as to invent something I couldn't control.'

'My parents were poisoned, though,' said Victor. 'No one wanted to buy any of the inventions so he put something in our water and it made everyone so sick they can't get out of bed. Could you help them too?'

'I think I know what he used,' said the woman. 'Another invention of mine, though not at all what you'd think.

It is also very easily fixable.'

'But we're still stuck here,' said Mingus. 'Even if you could help them, we can't get out.'

'Perhaps,' said the thin woman. 'Perhaps not. Could I get another look at that tortoise?'

'I don't think so,' said Victor, who suspected that the woman was so hungry that she wanted to eat Saint Oswald in his entirety.

The woman could see what he was thinking. 'I won't eat him, I promise you.'

'How do I know you won't?'

'I'm a vegetarian. We don't eat things that blink.'

The woman lumbered over to the tortoise. She crouched and ran a hand over his shell. Gently, she lifted him and felt the underside of his shell. Saint Oswald didn't seem upset by her touch. The thin woman nodded to herself wisely.

'It's as I thought,' the woman said. 'She's a Blackriver Nomad, from the Great Rolling Gorge. Incredibly rare, impossibly valuable. You ought to be extremely careful with her.'

'It's a "he", actually,' said Victor. 'He's called Saint Oswald.'

'No,' said the woman. 'She's a she: the underside of her shell is convex, not concave. You see, in females they bulge slightly in order to make room for eggs.' Victor's mouth fell open in shock. 'Now,' continued the woman. 'Do you know what unique property all Blackriver Nomads possess?'

None of the children had an answer.

'Their poo,' explained the thin woman, 'is highly explosive.'

16

It did not take long for spirits in the dungeon to lift. The children quickly let go of any reservations they had about the thin woman and they joined her in trying to work out the best plan of escape.

Should they try to blow apart the bars or the wall? How would they stop the moat rushing in? Or themselves from being caught in the blast? And how would they make it through the castle? Where would they go after that?

'We're right beside the water,' said Mo-Lan. 'That's why it's so damp in here. There's no way we can blow a hole in the wall without drowning ourselves.'

'She's right,' said the thin woman. 'Unfortunately, we shall have to venture back out through the castle, which we'd need to do anyway in order to track down my suitcase and the deactivators. Which will be a problem, as the explosion will draw attention.'

'Nah,' said Elena. 'The bartender at The Dozy Pony said people hear explosions going off here all the time.'

'You're right!' said the thin woman. 'It'll only sound like Walter tinkering with another one of his inventions.'

'So no one will notice?'

'They shouldn't do, not unless Walter realises that something's blowing up and he isn't the cause. If we're careful, we should be able to be far from this place before they notice we're gone.'

'What about the army?'

'Most of the army isn't in the castle. They're in barracks outside of town being trained. By the time he can set any of them on us, we should be deep in the arms of the city. I imagine you'll all be safe once you're home and we've sorted out your parents.'

'Before we start,' said Victor to the thin woman. 'What should we call you?'

'You can call me by my name,' said the thin woman. 'Polina.'

They waited three hours for Saint Oswald to poo. Once she'd done so, they took the poo in their hands and pressed it around two of the bars of the cell. Everyone collected scraps of string from the floor and these scraps were tied together into a fuse, one end of which was pressed into the tortoise poo. All that was left after that was to move as far away from the bars as possible and prepare to set fire to the end of the string.

'Ready?' said Polina.

The children nodded, all pressing their hands to their ears.

Polina took a tiny shard of mirror from the folds of her cloak. She held it an angle, reflecting the single ray of light that had struggled into the dungeon toward the tip of the fuse. A few seconds later, it was glowing red. Faint coils of smoke climbed into the air.

'That is what my invention is for,' Polina said. 'Not for looking at your own face.'

A flicker of flame raced along the fuse toward the bars.

For a moment, the world froze, before exploding in a thousand different colours. Everyone was blinded by white light and fantastic heat. Billowing smoke filled the dungeon. Polina ran toward it, flapping her hands to clear the air.

'It worked!' she called. 'Quick, we'd best get moving.'

They helped each other through the gap between the bars.

'Oz,' whispered Victor. 'You never told me you could do that, and you never said you were a girl.'

'*Uk*, *uk*,' said Saint Oswald.

'You're right, I guess it doesn't matter.'

They hurried up the stairs and along a dank corridor. Polina stuck her head through every doorway they passed, searching for her property. They passed no butlers or guards. It was beginning to feel as though the castle had been deserted.

Then, around one corner, they glimpsed a line of soldiers, shuffling forward along a corridor in single file. The soldiers all wore full suits of clanking armour, which they hadn't quite mastered the art of walking in. They seemed to be new recruits, who staggered like children in high heels.

And there was no way past them. Polina and the children crouched to wait. If they could only keep silent for long enough, then the soldiers would be gone and they could cross over into the main hall of the castle.

'Can anyone hear that?' asked Victor.

Soon enough, everyone could. Another group of soldiers was advancing behind them.

'We're trapped!' whispered Mingus. 'They're going to catch us and kill us and we won't ever get to go back home and save our parents and make them promise never to buy stupid things from mad pedlars.'

'We can't take on that many,' admitted Elena, who hadn't even bothered to reach for her bow.

'*Uk, uk*,' said Saint Oswald.

'Let me think,' said Mo-Lan.

'We don't have time to think!' said Elena.

'We don't have time for anything,' said Mingus.

'I have an idea,' said Mo-Lan.

Mo-Lan rushed forward to shove the stumbling soldier who was bringing up the rear. For a second, he teetered on the spot. The children held their breath. Finally, after what felt like an impossible amount of time, the soldier fell forward and all of those in front of him toppled like dominos. The hall filled with the sound of clattering metal and bawling men.

The five escapees were free to carry on their way out of the castle.

'That was amazing,' whispered Elena.

'Thank you,' answered Mo-Lan, her face breaking into a tiny smile.

They hurried on.

Polina soon found her old suitcase in an unguarded chamber that seemed to be Walter Swizwit's office. Thick ledgers lined the walls. Bored spiders sat in the ceiling corners.

As it had already been looted of anything that could make money, Walter Swizwit had not given much thought to the suitcase. It sat on a shelf under a blanket of dust. He had looked into it once, but the contraptions inside had made no sense to him and he couldn't work out a way of turning them into money. Besides, Polina's first three inventions had proven more than enough to amass great wealth.

Polina patted the case like an old friend. She slung it on to her back and led the children on to the main door.

Just as her hand reached for the door, a loud cackle erupted behind them.

'Did you really think you could simply walk out of the castle of the greatest inventor ever to set foot in this land?'

Polina and the four children turned to find Walter Swizwit standing at the top of the grand staircase. He was dressed in a flowing, fluffy robe, his hair still covered in bubbles from his fourth bath of the day. In his left hand he held what looked like a short, black club, with metal prongs protruding from its end.

Polina tried the door but it was locked. 'I've been in this castle for too long,' she said. 'You have no right to keep me here any longer.'

'You'd be cold and starving if it wasn't for me,' said Walter, who pretended to look hurt. 'If it wasn't for my hospitality, you'd be lying in a ditch, clutching your old bag of pointless garbage.'

Polina narrowed her eyes. 'I know you took my inventions

and sold them as your own.'

'Nonsense,' said Walter, advancing on the five of them, the device in his hand held aloft. 'Did the inventor of the wheel also invent the cart? Did the one who crafted the first brick build the first palace? I took your useless creations and turned them into something you could never have dreamed of. I used your paltry little bricks to build an empire.'

Walter Swizwit stopped a few metres from the children. He smelled of flowery soap and rancid butter. With his free hand, Walter patted his belly as though he'd just finished a feast.

'What do we do?' whispered Mingus.

'We fight,' said Elena. 'All of us, together.'

'That's sweet,' said Walter, his face splitting into a smile that showcased his shining teeth. 'But there won't be any more horseplay this afternoon.' He waved the device above his head. 'This,' he announced, 'is the Entrapinator. Unlike anything that woman has ever come up with, it is a creation that will change everything. No one will be capable of escaping its clutches. No one will ever be capable of disobeying me again.'

With a flourish, Walter flicked a switch on the device.

Great lengths of rope spurted from the end of the rod. They flailed madly against the walls of the hall so that it looked as though Walter was holding the hand of a panicked octopus. Walter was hoisted off his feet. The ropes tore burning torches from the walls and ripped banners in two and gouged deep scars in the stone walls.

The four children dropped to the floor, covering their heads with their hands.

Above them, the ropes whooshed through the air, as chandeliers smashed, statues fell and paintings crashed to the ground.

Walter howled like a dog greeting a full moon.

Eventually, everything fell silent.

The children hesitantly opened their eyes and got to their feet.

Walter Swizwit had been completely bound by the ropes of his invention. From his head to his feet, the cords of the Entrapinator had wrapped themselves around him so that not even a single centimetre of his soft pink skin was visible. The only sign of his continued existence was a muffled squeak coming from somewhere inside the coil of rope.

Polina let out a tiny laugh.

'I knew it,' she said. 'He isn't an inventor at all. He's a thief and a liar and a man who spends far too long in the bath.' She nodded at the children. 'We'd best get going while we still can.'

Using a sliver of smashed chandelier, Polina picked the lock of the door and let them out.

It was when they were halfway along the drawbridge that the first cries of alarm went up.

'Escaped prisoners!' came the cry from high above. 'Prisoners escaped from the dungeon!'

'Hurry,' urged Polina.

Clanking bells rang from the castle towers as Walter Swizwit's men were ordered to head out in pursuit of the prisoners. They picked up weapons and marched across the drawbridge, their heavy footsteps sending ripples through the cloudy water of the moat.

Soon, the children and Polina had the entire castle at their back.

17

Polina led them swiftly through the back streets of the city. Having spent her childhood playing hide-and-seek across Kaftan Minor, she knew every narrow alley and rooftop. She knew that the sewer between the town hall and the goose-girl statue was dry. She knew that there was a secret doorway below the Molehill Bridge. And she knew that you could jump from the bank to the plaza roof, but not back again.

'Quick,' she'd say, 'this way,'

and

'You'll have to crawl through here, watch your head,'

and

'Jump, but don't look down.'

As the morning birds woke up and sang their breakfast songs, the children followed the real inventor deep into the heart of the oldest part of town. The sun broke across the city, lining chimneypots with seams of gold and picking out specks of glitter in the roof tiles.

Polina finally stopped outside a crumbling, wood-frame house, wedged in the gap between a butcher's and a bookshop. She closed her eyes and breathed in. It smelt of fresh blood and old paper.

'Home,' she whispered. 'It's been a long while since I've seen you.'

Inside, the house had frozen in time. A thick layer of dust lay on top of everything. Books sat open, dirty plates were piled up in the sink. Polina gazed sadly at a half-finished bowl of mouldy breakfast that sat on the kitchen table. Watching her, Victor wondered how long it had been since she'd seen her home. Had she felt the same way he'd done over a week ago, waking up to a normal day only to have everything turn upside down? How long would it be before he saw his home again?

They climbed the three rickety staircases that led to the roof. There, a huge tarpaulin was draped over something big enough to be a boat.

'What is it?' asked Victor.

'Help me get the cover off and you'll find out.'

Together, they heaved the sheet to one side.

The construction that was revealed to them was a kind of

wooden plane consisting of a cabin mounted with a sofa and an armchair, two pairs of red wings, and a central torch fixed to a cloth balloon. It looked as though it had been built with pieces of scrap pilfered from junkyards.

'A balloon-assisted biplane,' said Mo-Lan in amazement. 'I've never seen one before. I was almost sure they didn't exist.'

'They didn't,' said Polina. 'Until I invented them.'

'What's the balloon for?' asked Elena, wrinkling her nose and prodding the shrivelled sack of cloth.

'It allows you to take off without the need for a runway,' explained Polina. 'The balloon will get us in the air then we'll jump-start the propeller and get ourselves really moving.'

At seeing the plane, Polina's face had brightened. Her skin no longer seemed so paper-white and her cheeks had filled out slightly. She bounced around the machine, checking various catches and latches, and nodding seriously to herself.

'It also means we can land far more precisely,' she said. 'We fire the balloon up while we're in the air, cut the propeller, and then lower ourselves to exactly the place we want to be.'

'Is it safe?' asked Mingus. 'It looks like it's about to fall apart.'

'Of course it's safe,' said Polina. 'I don't build things that don't last. Now, everyone, hop in. You might have to sit on each other's laps.'

It was a tight squeeze but they managed to fit. Victor held Saint Oswald on his lap, Elena sat on top of Mo-Lan, and Mingus managed to squash himself into a small compartment that was intended for luggage.

'Everyone ready?'

'Yes,' said Victor.

'No,' said Mingus.

'Then let's go,' said Polina.

Polina set alight the central torch and adjusted its dial. A jet of flame roared toward the sky. In no time, the fire had filled the balloon with hot air, and the plane began to lift off the ground. It teetered in the air, like a boat on choppy waters, but didn't seem in danger of falling out of the sky.

As they rose up, the children could see men trooping through the streets of the city. Hundreds of them swarmed like ants around the buildings. There were already soldiers at the door of Polina's house. They threw the heels of their boots at it, screaming for the escaped prisoners to hand themselves over.

'My poor door,' whispered Polina. 'I suppose I'll never see my home again.'

She reached forward and yanked on a cord that set the propeller spinning. The plane lurched forward. Its pilot leaned back in her seat and directed her flying creation through the rosy morning clouds.

18

They soared over the city of Kaftan Minor and the fields around it, rising higher and higher until all that they could see below them were banks of white fluff.

'We're not going straight into the woods,' Polina explained, shouting through the rushing air. 'It's too close, they'll see where we're heading and follow us there. We need to shake them off first.'

Once they'd travelled some way, she dipped down, and burst back through the clouds.

The kids gasped.

A world they had never imagined unfolded below them.

Other cities passed by, grander cities, with taller spires and streets that were still bustling with people. They saw deep canyons of orange rock and waterfalls that split the sunlight into rainbows. Trees as crooked as ancient folk raised their skinny arms to the sky. Lone thunderclouds ranged like floating fish over the land.

Victor felt his heart lift. This was what he'd once dreamt of, standing on the smallest mountain with his giant tortoise. This was the wide world, where history was written and discoveries were made.

Polina lowered the plane and skimmed them across a lake of water so still you might mistake it for a mirror.

She wove them through the peaks of a precarious mountain range.

And then, in the distance, the children saw a small, dark fortress that stuck out on the landscape like an ink blot. A river of filthy water roared around its perimeters. Smears of grimy fog hung above it.

'What was that place?' asked Mo-Lan.

Polina flew back to give them another look at the dark settlement, making sure not to draw too close. It was smaller than any of the cities, but starker. All around it, the trees had been cleared. The ground looked scorched, as though a fierce and sudden fire had burnt away all the life that had once covered it. A single, straight, crumbling path led from the looming iron gates of the city into the woods that surrounded it.

'That,' she said, 'is the place where the collectors dwell. It is not a place anyone can visit. You do not come to the collectors, they come to you.'

'They have an entire city?'

'They do. The ones that have visited you are only a small fraction of the whole. There are many of them, more than you could imagine. Rumour has it that they sleep on cold stone floors, using their own hands as pillows.'

'But they're just people?' said Victor, who felt like the only one who still had no real idea what a collector was. 'You make them sound like monsters.'

'They were people once,' said Polina. 'Until they lost their hearts to money. You have all suffered under their system of debt. The collectors roam out to distant corners of the land and offer food or tools to people who are desperately in need of them. Those people then pay them back, bit by bit, but there is a catch: the longer it takes them to pay back the money, the more money they owe. I've not yet met a single person who's managed to climb out from under them.'

Not for the first time, Victor wondered, guiltily, why it was that the villages of his friends had all fallen under the power of the collectors when Rainwater had managed to escape. What made his village special? Why didn't any of the people there owe anything to the collectors?

'Look,' said Mo-Lan, pointing down at the walled city.

As they watched, a door swung open in the gloomy castle and ten hooded figures on black horses thundered out. They all rode hunched forward, as though great weights were pressing down on their backs. Giant saddlebags hung from either side of each horse. The creatures carried their riders with such speed that they were hardly more than smudges on the landscape.

'I've never seen so many,' whispered Mingus.

'That's a lot of them, true enough,' said Polina. 'Must be a big debt they're off to collect.'

The children shivered at the thought, each imagining their own homes being dismantled and carried away. What would be left of their villages by the time they returned to them? Anything? Anyone?

'Polina?' asked Mo-Lan. 'What exactly did you mean earlier when you said if your time belongs to others you stop valuing it?'

'I meant what I said,' said the inventor. 'It ruins people to feel as though their time is not their own. Every waking moment is invaded with worry. To live in debt is to live in a shadow. It's why I can't understand how the king could ever allow the collectors to operate as they do in the first place.'

All of a sudden, the plane dove headfirst into a dark cloud. The children pawed at the crystals of ice that latched on to their eyebrows and fringes.

When they emerged, all of them were soaked. They

blinked at each other. Mo-Lan fished a scrap of white out of Mingus's hair.

'Well?' said Elena.

Mingus sighed, the big, long sigh of someone who was about to agree to something he very much did not want to do. 'We can't go home yet, can we?'

'If we go back now,' said Mo-Lan, 'we'll soon find ourselves in the same situation as our parents, with no possibility of ever getting out.'

'Exactly,' said Elena. 'All I'll ever do is mine stupid rubies.'

'And they'll force me to go hunting every day,' moaned Mingus.

'And I'll never be allowed to stop thinking,' said Mo-Lan, pulling on her hair.

Victor felt the wind whip a tear out of the corner of his eye. He leant out of the plane and squinted down at the ugly city below. He had an idea. 'Polina,' he said. 'How do the collectors know how much everyone owes them?'

'They keep records,' she said. 'It is said that they have a huge hall filled with detailed records of everything they are owed by all the people in their debt.'

'Okay,' said Victor. 'What would happen if those records disappeared?'

'Theoretically,' said Mo-Lan, her eyes widening in

excitement, 'they wouldn't have any proof that anyone owed them anything.'

'She's right,' said Polina. 'If they didn't have records, then they wouldn't be able to prove that anyone in any of your villages had borrowed from them and so they wouldn't be able to collect or take people away as payment.'

'You really think they'd stop?'

'They'd have to,' said Polina. 'Even the collectors couldn't face off against the king's army. They may be powerful but even they aren't outside the law.'

The children all looked at each other.

'Do you think it's possible?' said Mingus. 'Could we really sneak in and find a way to destroy the records? What if they caught us? What if they chained us up and tortured us and forced us to survive on only very small pies and water?'

'They won't catch us,' said Elena, her hair flying in the wind.

'It's highly probable that they might,' added Mo-Lan. 'But it's not certain.'

Victor took that to mean they were both in. 'Polina,' he said. 'Will you help us get in there and destroy the records?'

The inventor paused for a moment. 'It is at least partly my fault that you're in this situation, so I don't see that I can refuse your request. But you should know that the people in that fortress are not people like you or me. The only thing they have a feeling for is money. If they catch us, they won't think twice about locking us away and forgetting us completely.' She shifted a handful of red hair from out of her eyes. 'And Walter will not forget us either. Once his soldiers have cut him out of his cocoon, he'll come looking. It's likely he's already on his way. They might not bother with you children, but he won't be able to risk having me on the loose.'

'We'll protect you,' said Elena seriously.

'We will,' promised Victor.

Mingus nodded. 'Even if it means they catch us again.'

'It'll just mean we have to concoct another escape plan,' said Mo-Lan.

The inventor chuckled. 'That's very kind of you all,' she said. 'Let's hope it doesn't come to that.'

Polina steered the plane over to a small clearing in the trees. She slowly shrunk the flame that was keeping the balloon aloft so that they were lowered gently on to the ground. It was dark in the shade of the trees. With trepidation, they climbed out of the plane.

19

'So,' asked Victor, once they'd all arranged a makeshift camp. 'First we'll need to come up with a plan for how to get in.'

'It will be difficult,' said Polina. 'They do not let anyone who is not of their kind enter. Many come, in search of their relatives who have been take away as payment. But none are allowed to pass through the iron gates.'

'Could we fly in?' said Mo-Lan.

'It wouldn't work,' said Polina. 'They keep lookouts stationed along the walls of the fortress. As soon as they saw us approaching, they'd shoot the plane down with flaming arrows.'

'Could we dig?' said Mingus.

Polina shook her head. 'Their walls go too deep,' she explained. 'The amount of treasure they're hoarding in that place, they wouldn't leave a thing like that to chance. You'd sooner dig a tunnel under the Eastern Ocean than you could dig one under the wall of the dark fortress.'

'What if they thought we were collectors?' said Elena.

'Right,' said Mo-Lan. 'Is it possible that we might somehow disguise ourselves as their kind? With that method, we may well fool the guards into letting us pass. Of course there's the possibility that disguises might prove insufficient, in which case they could very well—' She pulled on her hair and stopped talking.

'We'd have to steal them from real collectors,' said Mingus, not looking thrilled at the prospect. 'And I don't think we should get too close to them. Whenever I get close to them, the gap between my shoulder blades starts itching and I feel like I'm going to faint.'

'You'll be okay,' said Victor. 'We'll be with you.'

The boy from the hunting town didn't look convinced.

'That may well be our only hope,' said Polina. 'And I may well have an idea for how to manage it. We will have to rely on the element of surprise. And we will have to wait until night falls. Do you all know how to ride horses?'

'No,' said Elena.

'Not yet,' said Victor.

'Theoretically, I do,' said Mo-Lan. 'Horses are quadrupeds that eat grass. I have read about them, though I've never come across one in real life.'

'I know horses,' said Mingus. 'We ride out on them sometimes to hunt. The secret is to treat them like you'd treat someone you like very much but you're a little bit scared of. You should never say anything mean or tell them off. If they're worried, you whisper to them. And if you want them to go fast, you tickle behind their ears.'

'Did everyone hear that?' said Polina. 'That was sound advice and you'd do well to heed it.'

As night fell, the forest came to life, but the sounds it rang with were nothing like the sounds that floated into the children's villages at night. The forest howled and cried and whispered. It spoke sad words and screamed angry ones. The trees hurled rocks and dirt and leaves. For hours, things thumped the ground and whistled through the air.

The sounds grew and grew. They became almost deafening. Huddled around the campfire, the children and the inventor trembled with fear. They were sipping what was left of Victor's tea, but it wasn't enough to stop their thoughts from conjuring up the most hideous monsters.

For some reason, Victor's mind drifted back to the frozen people and animals in the Rock of Little Regard. He felt almost guilty, leaving them behind like that. Was there anything they could have done to help? Or would they be stuck, unmoving in the lonely gloom for ever?

'Polina,' he said. 'Have you ever heard of the Iron Plague?'

'Of course,' said the inventor. 'It shaped our world. Had it not cleared the face of the kingdom all those years ago, there would be ten times as many people living under King Marshalla today. I've heard it said that were it not for the plague, we'd have a city as big as every village between the two seas combined.'

Victor sighed. Maybe, he thought, if there'd never been a stupid plague, he'd have grown up in a city too, surrounded by books and music and beautiful objects that did nothing in particular. 'If someone had been turned to metal, could you turn them back?'

Polina shook her head. 'No,' she said. 'I'm sorry, it's not possible. Metal isn't like ice; it doesn't preserve, it replaces.'

The sounds raged until, dead in the middle of the night, everything suddenly went completely silent.

The children looked at each other.

'What's happening?' asked Mingus.

Polina raised a finger to her lips. She stood up and stamped out the fire before waving for the children to follow her and crouch, waiting, between the trees at the edge of the road.

It wasn't long before they could see the distant shadows of a band of collectors thundering along the road.

20

Before the collectors drew close enough to glimpse them, they split into two groups and took positions at either side of the road. On one side, Polina, Mingus and Mo-Lan held an end of rope, while on the other, Victor and Elena gripped its opposite end. They all crouched low to the ground so that the rope across the road lay flat and invisible.

The hooves of the collectors' horses grew louder and louder. They shook the leaves on the trees. Night birds scattered into the sky. Glowbugs hurried back into the fallen trunks they called home.

From across the road, Victor could just about see the whites of the inventor's eyes in the moonlight. He saw her raise three fingers and slowly fold them away as the collectors approached.

Three.

Two.

One.

Both sides pulled tight on the ends of the rope so that it flew into the air.

And the three collectors fell from their horses, landing with dull thumps on the dusty road. Before they had a chance to get to their feet and figure out what was going on, the children had raced in, leapt on to their backs, and begun scrabbling to tie their hands in knots.

'Tie them quickly,' said Polina. 'Don't let them get to their feet.'

Both Mingus and Mo-Lan each fell directly on top of a collector as the inventor rushed to bind their hands and feet.

'You are making a grave mistake,' said one of the cloaked men who had been tackled to the ground by Victor and Elena. 'Others of our kind will notice when we fail to return. They will come looking.'

Up close, Victor still had no idea how the collectors looked. Their black cloaks reached all the way to the ground and the hoods hung so far forward on their heads that their faces were lost in shadow.

'Take his arms,' shouted Elena.

'I can't find his arms,' said Victor.

They were both attempting to keep the man pinned down

while simultaneously trying to pull his hands behind his back.

'Got you,' Victor muttered.

As he pulled the man's arm out from the folds of black cloth, Victor recoiled at the sight of the spindly blue arm he was clutching. The skin was so pale as to be translucent and he could see the network of blue and green veins and arteries criss-crossing beneath it. Tattooed on to the skin were endless chains of numbers that wound around the arms like vines. The collector was cold to the touch and his skin reminded Victor of uncooked meat.

'You underestimate our reach,' hissed the cloaked man.

'Oh, shut up,' said Elena.

'You will pay for your words.'

'Actually, no one's ever going to pay you again.'

Victor yelped as the collector rolled to one side, shaking off both him and Elena. Elena lunged to tackle him but it was too late. He'd already jumped to his feet, reached inside his cloak and produced a small dagger shaped like a crescent moon.

'Please,' Victor said, covering his face with his hands. 'Don't hurt me. I haven't done anything.'

The collector turned to Polina and pointed at the two collectors that were kneeling, tied up, on the ground. 'Untie them,' he said. 'Now. Or I'll hurt the boy.'

Both Polina and Mo-Lan grudgingly untied the men they'd just managed to wrest control of. They did it as slowly as possible, as though hoping something would happen to rescue them from the situation before it was too late. As they unpicked their knots, Mingus stood shaking to one side. All of the colour had fallen out of his face.

'Now tie up those children you came with,' the collector with the dagger said to Polina.

'No!' said Mingus. 'Please, please, please, please. I absolutely hate being tied up.'

The collector snarled. 'Do the loud, scared one first.'

Polina hesitated.

The collector moved his knife closer to Victor's neck.

'Do it,' he insisted.

With tears in her eyes, Polina set about tying up Mingus, Mo-Lan and Elena. She started with Mingus, whispering that she was sorry before wrapping the rope around his wrists and linking the ends in the loosest possible knot she could muster.

'Now the others,' ordered the collector.

Victor flinched as the glinting blade passed back and forth in front of his eyes. He watched as the inventor tied up Mo-Lan and started worked on Elena.

Suddenly, the horses of the collectors let out wild cries of alarm, rearing up wildly.

Polina's hands let get go of the rope she'd looped around Elena's wrists.

'Easy,' said one of the collectors, trying to calm the panicked animals. 'Easy, boys. It's okay.'

The horses either didn't listen or didn't believe their masters. They blew jets of steam from their nostrils and galloped away in the opposite direction to the dark fortress. Soon enough they had disappeared from sight.

'What was that?' screamed the collector with the dagger. 'What spooked the beasts?'

Which was when Mingus shrieked with fright.

And the dagger fell from Victor's neck.

All around them, pale green people were climbing down from the trees.

21

The people who climbed down from the trees were dressed in ill-fitting clothes put together from scraps of cloth, bark and large leaves. Their skin had a slight greenish glow so that they gave off their own eerie light that lit up the ground around where they stood. They were clearly humans, but humans that looked to have spent so long in the forest that it had started to become a part of them. Moss freckled their faces and lichen hung from their ears. Their fingernails were the colour of sunken ships.

There must have been hundreds of them.

They surrounded the group of collectors and the children without hurry, barely making a sound. None of the people had any weapons. They all wore peaceful, calm expressions on their faces.

'Who are you?' said the collector, swinging his dagger. A moment earlier it had seemed like a terrible, dangerous

weapon, but in the presence of the people from the trees it looked small and useless. 'Leave us be. You needn't get mixed up in this.'

'We are already mixed up in this,' said the people in unison.

'Who am I speaking to? Who are you demons? Identify yourselves.'

One man stepped out from the mass of people. He was slightly taller than the others and had a green beard that stretched from his chin to the ground. Leaves, twigs and even the nest of a bird were snagged in the wiry hair that grew from his face and trailed along behind him as he walked.

'I am Greenbeard,' he said. 'And we are the people in the trees. We are people who have come from cities ten thousand leagues away. Some of us come from across the Eastern Ocean, from the Old West, and from the Northern Reaches. All of us came here when you took the ones we loved most, simply because we could not manage to give you the vast sums and resources you demanded.'

'Those are the rules,' said the collector, his voice wavering. 'We didn't make them.'

'They are not the rules of nature,' said the man. 'They are simply your own rules, rules that you put in place to benefit yourselves. You created a world in which our lives are lived in service to you. No matter how hard we worked, our lives did not get better; it was only you who reaped the rewards.'

'It wasn't us who started it,' pleaded the collector.

'It does not matter if you lit the fire,' said Greenbeard. 'It matters that you kept the fire burning, even as it caused so much misery for so many.'

Three of the green folk strode forward and stripped the cloaks from the collectors.

The men beneath them were tiny and frail looking. To make their bodies appear larger than they really were, the collectors wore big wooden frames around their chests that their cloaks were draped over. Without the cover of their dark capes, they looked like children stuck in barrels, their tiny arms and legs flailing uselessly. Their heads were shaven and bulbous compared to their bodies, and the tattoos Victor had glimpsed running up one of their arms covered every inch of their pale skins.

The tree people passed out the cloaks to Victor, Mingus and Elena.

'You'll be needing those if you're to gain entry to their fortress,' said Greenbeard. 'There will be more cloaks packed on the horses; we shall make sure you get those too.'

'Were you watching us this whole time?' Victor said. 'You could hear us?'

'I'm afraid we were,' said the man with the green beard. 'We had to make sure you were friends. There are many enemies in these woods. As you have found out.'

Greenbeard turned his face to the shivering collectors. 'Take them away,' he said. 'Hold them for three days and then release them. They will then face a choice: to return to their old lives or to head into the world and carve out new ones. We can do nothing but give them a chance to change.'

The collectors struggled as the people in the trees dragged them away.

Greenbeard helped Victor up. He took the dagger from the ground, broke it in two, and hurled the two shards into the air. As though it had been waiting, a crow swooped out of nowhere and snatched up the gleaming slivers of metal in its beak. Victor could have sworn he heard the bird squawk 'Thank you'.

Something about Greenbeard's presence made him relax. Standing by him made Victor feel as though he was at home, tucked up in bed, being sung to sleep by his mother. The thought of her brought tears to his eyes. They were so far away from each other. And if he hadn't agreed to go to the fortress with Elena, Mingus and Mo-Lan, he could have been home by now, saving them with the inventor's help. But surely they'd want him to help his friends and their families?

Surely they'd understand?

The man spoke as though he could read Victor's mind. 'Don't fear,' he said. 'They know that you are doing all you can for the greater good.'

Four of the tree people came skipping down the road toward them. They were holding the reins of the collectors' spooked horses, whispering gently to them in order to get them to calm down.

'You will not leave for the castle tonight,' Greenbeard said. 'It is too much of a risk for what you have planned. You will sleep with us in the trees and tomorrow you will ride into the dark fortress. The collectors' horses will be calmer by then. And please, accept one of our own steeds to help you on your way.'

The people from the trees climbed expertly back up into the canopy and helped the four children and the inventor up after them. Victor was amazed to see that they had constructed their own village high up in the forest. There were houses built into the trees, put together from parts of old carts and odd windows and branches bound together with rope. The haphazard buildings were linked together by rickety walkways and long ladders that formed a criss-crossing network through the canopy.

On a wooden platform that hung between several sturdy

oaks, the children sat among the tree people and the small fire they kept burning in a large rock shaped like a bowl. Their hosts moved slowly and quietly and rarely talked among themselves. Instead, they seemed to spend their time staring at things: droplets of water on leaves, the palms of their own hands or bugs on tree bark.

'So all of you have relatives who were taken by the collectors?' asked Elena.

'Yes,' said Greenbeard. 'We all came here seeking a way of getting them back. We were each turned away at the gates but could not bring ourselves to abandon those we loved entirely. Instead we chose to remain as close to them as possible.'

'Is it you making all those scary sounds?' asked Mingus.

'I'm afraid it is,' Greenbeard told him. 'You see, night time is when we gather around the walls of the fortress and call out to the ones we have lost. We throw in parcels of food too, and notes and photographs to remind them of home, though we have no way of knowing whether any of our messages get through.'

'Why do you go at night?' Polina wanted to know.

'If we went in the day, they'd be able to pick us off with arrows. It is only under the cover of darkness that we can call to them in safety.' Greenbeard lifted his large, dirty hand.

'But that is enough sad talk. Our lives here are spent in quiet hopelessness. For now, we have visitors, and this is a rare and splendid occasion. So let us eat. Let us eat well.'

On cue, green people began swinging in and landing on the platform, bringing with them steaming bowls of fruits and vegetables, most of which Victor failed to recognise. There were glistening buns packed with jackfruit and tiny diamond-shaped sandwiches filled with moonflowers. There were soups that tasted like rain hitting dry ground. There were soft noodles as long as skipping ropes and shivering jellies that smelled like summer berries.

The children ate until they felt ready to burst. As they ate, the new flavours melting into their tongues, they were briefly transported away from their dangerous, hopeless situation. The food gave them a break from their worry.

After everyone had eaten, a man swung on to the platform, panting.

'Elena?' he said, staggering over to a shocked Elena. 'Our Elena? Is that really you? I came as soon as I heard. They told me someone with your name was here but I couldn't bring myself to believe it was you. Is it? Tell me, is it you?'

'Uncle,' said Elena, leaping up to hug the relative she thought she'd never see again. 'We thought you'd disappeared for ever,' she said.

'I just couldn't bear to leave her,' said the man. 'I couldn't leave your aunt alone in that horrible dark place.'

'It's okay,' Elena said. 'I understand.'

'You're really here,' said the uncle. 'Tell me, how is Moonwald?'

Elena shook her head. 'Not good. That's why we're here. We're going to make things right again.'

Greenbeard cleared his throat and stood up. All of the green people stopped speaking and turned to face him.

'Now,' he said. 'We know that you are going into the fortress to destroy the records. But we would also like to make another request of you, if we may. We would ask that you do whatever you can to try to free our loved ones too. We would have tried doing such a thing many moons ago, but the collectors warned us that they would punish our loved ones if we did.'

'Of course we will,' said Elena, letting go of her uncle and stepping close to Greenbeard.

'We'll try, at least,' said Victor.

'That is all we can ask,' said Greenbeard. He gestured for everyone to start moving away from the platform. 'But first you must sleep,' he said. 'People are beasts without a good night's sleep.'

The four children and the inventor slept soundly in the

canopy of the forest. As they snored, the people in the trees mixed a special blend of herbs and feathers over the embers of the fire. It was a potent mixture, concocted specially to ensure that those who smelled it dreamed only the sweetest and most peaceful dreams.

For the people in the trees, dreams were more important than almost anything else. Their dreams were the only places in which they could see those people who had been taken from them by the collectors. Dreams were what kept them going on even the coldest nights.

Even Saint Oswald dreamed well. As she snored inside her shell, the giant tortoise saw herself riding serenely across a still ocean on the back of a giant lettuce leaf.

22

Victor was nudged awake by Elena. When he opened his eyes, he saw her hovering over him, a finger pressed to her lips.

'Shh,' she said. 'Everyone else is still sleeping. I just thought you'd want to see.'

'See what?' he said, rubbing his half-open eyes.

'Stand up.'

He stood and their heads burst through the ceiling of leaves.

Victor gasped.

The tops of the trees spread out like a rippling sea of deep green around them. In the distance, the sun was breaking over the horizon, its half-circle of white light looking like the dome of a grand cathedral from another world. The sky behind it was a charged electric blue.

'It's amazing,' he said.

'I know,' said Elena. 'I never realised the sun was that big.'

'At home,' Victor told her, 'I used to rush to the top of the hill every morning so I could see the sun rise. I'd always imagine how the same sun was looking over the big, exciting cities, where things were actually happening, and I'd wish so hard that I'd get chance to see them.'

'And now what do you think?'

'That I'd quite like to be at home.'

Elena laughed. 'It's stupid, isn't it? I used to feel the same. Like Moonwald was the most boring place and I wanted to be anywhere else.'

'Exactly,' said Victor.

'Now we're actually where things are happening,' said Elena.

'And things happening is quite scary,' said Victor. 'I wouldn't mind if things stopped happening now.'

Reluctantly, they both disappeared back under the leaves once they could hear everyone waking up. On the wooden platform, they came across Mingus and Mo-Lan sitting side by side, both perfectly still and with their eyes closed. They looked like a pair of statues. For a moment, Victor panicked that the Iron Plague had somehow taken them. Then Mingus's left hand twitched.

Elena and Victor both looked at each other and shrugged.

Neither of them had any idea what was going on.

They sidled closer to their unmoving friends.

'Pssst,' said Elena. 'Are you two sleeping sitting up?'

Mingus opened one eye.

'No,' he said. 'We're being cool, calm lakes.'

'What?'

'We were meditating,' said Mo-Lan, opening both her eyes and sighing. 'Greenbeard taught us. But you've ruined it now.'

'What's the point of it?' asked Elena, taking a seat opposite the girl from Sektun-Layley.

Mingus stood up and shook the stiffness out of his legs. 'Greenbeard said that the people in the trees learned how to do it because otherwise they'd end up spending all their time thinking about their families and they'd never not be sad.'

'So they discovered a method for training their thoughts,' explained Mo-Lan. 'With practice, you can make your head stop talking so much. You can make it sit still.'

Mingus beamed. 'He said I could use it to stop being afraid of everything.'

Mo-Lan nodded. 'And I can teach my brain to stop thinking so much that it gets tired.'

'You'll need a lot of practice first,' boomed Greenbeard,

appearing beside them as if from nowhere. 'And a bit of food.'

They shared a breakfast of fresh gallflower petals and mint tea before carefully descending from the canopy and on to the forest floor.

When it came to it, Victor, Elena, Mingus, Mo-Lan and Polina were sorry to say goodbye to the people in the trees but they knew that they had to destroy the records if they truly wanted to set their families free. And they also knew they didn't have much time left. If their parents stayed glued to the inventions much longer, they would either end up starving or being taken away by the collectors.

The children and the inventor dressed themselves in the cloaks of their enemies. Mingus winced as he put his on.

'It smells weird,' he said. 'Like old fish and that stuff you find in your bellybutton.'

'It's them,' said Elena. 'None of them smell right.'

Mo-Lan nodded. 'A combination of body odour and unfriendliness,' she suggested.

It was decided that Victor would wear a leather belt around his waist that would keep Saint Oswald strapped to him. As Mo-Lan had pointed out, there weren't many collectors wandering around with giant tortoises at their heels, and Saint Oswald was bound to be noticed if they ever managed to get past the fortress gates.

The tree people had gathered along the road to see them off.

Greenbeard gently stroked Victor's horse as two green people lifted him into the saddle. As soon as he was on the beast, he wanted to get off. He did not feel remotely comfortable sitting on the back of a horse.

'Ride well and stay safe,' said the man with the green beard. 'Try not to be afraid. They are nothing more than people who have lost their way. Though they may dress as darkness, they are nothing so terrifying as that.'

'Thank you for your help,' said Victor, trying to look calm on the back of the bucking animal.

'You will help us far more than we have helped you,' said Greenbeard. 'Now go.' He patted the horse and it burst into action, bolting forward as Victor struggled to stay on top of it.

Waving madly, the group trotted along the road toward the fortress. With the exception of Mingus, they all bounced about on top of the horses like jack-in-the-boxes. None of the animals listened to their squealed requests to slow down. In fact, it seemed like the louder they complained, the faster the animals decided to carry them.

'You have to relax,' Mingus shouted. 'Don't sit so straight.

Move with the horse. Not against it.'

After an hour of riding, they had scarcely improved. Both Victor and Mo-Lan had fallen off their horses and had to be helped back on. Mingus suggested to Mo-Lan that she try meditating while riding, rather than overthinking every tiny movement. After that, she rode more smoothly, and went on ahead at his side. Victor and Elena, on the other hand, hung on to their reins for dear life and almost breathed a sigh of relief when their destination loomed into view.

The shadow of the fortress fell over them long before they drew close. Victor wasn't sure if he was imagining it but it felt as though the temperature dropped. The sun above the trees already felt like a distant memory.

He shivered as they pulled up at the dark fortress. The animals didn't need to be told to stop. They automatically came to a halt as they neared the place where the collectors dwelt.

Its gates were ancient, vicious-looking slabs of metal. They were covered in dents and scratches and burns. Up close, Victor could make out tiny pieces of graffiti, carved into the rusty metal. He realised they were notes written by the people in the trees. WE WILL KEEP WAITING, read one. WE HAVE NOT FORGOTTEN, read another.

The shrouded faces of two guards peered from battlements

either side of the gate. They didn't say anything, just took in the group waiting below. The children and the inventor shifted nervously on their horses.

Mingus lifted a hand to wave.

Elena pulled it down before anyone had seen.

'Collectors don't wave,' she whispered.

They had been prepared to answer questions but none were put to them. Instead the gates swung open and the five intruders entered the dark fortress, four of them trying their best to look as though it wasn't the first time they'd come anywhere near a horse.

Only once they were through the gates did any of them breathe again.

23

The ground inside the walls of the fortress was black. The few collectors who wandered around did so while staring down, heavy bags clasped in their pale hands. Nobody spoke. The only sounds were the hush of footsteps and the far-off clink of metal against metal.

'How do you do?' said Mo-Lan, nodding to a passing collector.

'Shhh,' whispered Elena. 'They don't speak like that.'

The majority of the space within the fortress was taken up by three imposing buildings built of bricks so dark you couldn't see the seams of where they had been put together. The buildings were connected to each other and the only way in was a doorway in the smallest of the three. There were no windows in any of the structures. Their walls were sheer faces of the deepest black, like universes stripped of their stars.

Every now and again, a collector would bustle over to the doorway in the smallest of the three buildings and knock before being let in.

Around the large structure were a number of long, low cabins, also without windows, but with stubby chimneys that pumped dark smoke into the fresh morning.

'I think they sleep in the small buildings,' whispered Polina. 'The other three must be where they work.'

'Do you think the records are stored in one of them?'

'They must be,' said Polina. 'But they're probably keeping the records in the last building. I have no idea what could be in the first two, but we'll have to go through them to get there.'

The five of them trotted slowly forward on their horses, trying their best not to look suspicious, but having no real idea of where they ought to go or how they ought to behave. Mingus rode with his head bowed forward, Elena threw her shoulders back, and Mo-Lan tried to mimic the only other collector she could see by slightly swaying from side to side.

'You there!' called a voice. 'What do you think you're doing?'

Mingus clutched his heart in panic.

Elena stuck out her chin in defiance.

A man had appeared from nowhere and positioned

himself in front of them. Like everyone else, he wore a dark cloak, pulled low over his face, and heavy boots caked in mud. He stood before them with his hands on his hips. 'Beasts go in the stables,' barked the man. 'You can't go riding around inside the walls. You know the rules. Stable your animals then bring your takings to the counting hall.' He shook his head as he walked away. 'Honestly,' he muttered. 'No matter how many times I say it, folk are always thinking they can ride around willy nilly, this ain't a racetrack, it's a . . .'

Obediently, the five of them jumped off their horses. Victor landed awkwardly, falling to one side and landing with his hands in the black dirt. It felt like ash between his fingers. Mingus helped him and the tortoise up.

Luckily, just at that moment, they could see another pair of collectors ride in, leap off their horses and begin leading them toward one of the low buildings.

'Follow them,' whispered Polina.

They walked on behind the collectors and their horses. Both of the animals were weighed down with bulging saddlebags that looked to contain huge masses of heavy coins.

Inside the stable, the first two collectors hauled the bags off their horses and tied their animals to pegs in the wall.

'Best get takings over to the clerks sharpish,' one said. 'They're gettin' more and more tight, I swear.'

The five intruders stood back, attempting to keep themselves hidden behind their horses.

'We don't have takings,' whispered Mingus. 'Where are our takings? We're supposed to have takings.'

'Stop saying "takings",' said Elena.

'We could say we didn't get anything,' suggested Victor.

'But if we aren't in possession of coins,' said Mo-Lan, 'we'd be bringing people and unless any of you want to volunteer, we aren't going to have people to give them either.'

The two collectors spun about and eyed them suspiciously.

Polina stepped around her horse. 'They want you back at the gates,' she said, in a gruff voice. 'Best hurry off before they get too upset.'

'At the gates?' answered one of them. 'And why is that?'

'You dropped bags, I believe. You're to go and collect them quickly, or else you'll be docked.'

There was a moment of tension as the children waited to see whether the collectors would believe the lie.

Then one of them let out a deep sigh.

'I told you they weren't properly tied on,' he complained to his colleague.

'Wasn't my fault you can't tie knots,' his colleague replied.

'Well, neither can you apparently.'

'Well, I'm better than you.'

The two collectors departed, still bickering, and the children divided up the bags they'd left behind between themselves. Once they'd securely tied their horses, they hurried over to the door in the smallest building. Victor knocked and took a step back.

A hatch slid open and a large eye webbed with veins appeared.

'Bringing or taking?' said the eye.

'Uh,' said Victor. 'Bringing takings?'

'Which villages?'

'Moonwald,' said Elena.

'Aeldbird,' said Mingus.

'Sektun-Layley,' said Mo-Lan.

'And you two?' said the eye, aiming itself at Victor and Polina.

'Both Kaftan Minor,' said Polina. 'Lower Bognor Street and Ilyich Inn.'

'In you come then,' said the eye. 'Drop them with the clerks and get out. We can't have you dawdling too long.'

And the door swung open, revealing a vast and crowded hall, choked with smoke.

24

There were thousands upon thousands of desks filling the hall, each with someone hunched over it, scribbling hurriedly on to scraps of paper. The only light came from the stubs of small candles melted into the corners of the tables. Their tiny flames lit the endless rows of pained faces from beneath. The ceiling was so far above the huddled scribblers that Victor struggled to see to the top of it in the gloom.

'Look,' whispered Mingus, pointing toward the ground.

Victor cast his eyes down. Heavy metal manacles were fixed around the feet of the people at the desks, chaining them to the furniture they were writing on. The people were dressed in little more than rags. Their feet were bare and their faces looked gaunt.

In one corner of the room, perched on a high stool, a giant dressed in the largest cloak Victor had ever seen was snoring. He wore huge chains wrapped around his waist, with a key hanging from each link. A bulbous nose protruded from under his hood and each time the man exhaled, his breath sent the long black hairs of his nostrils fluttering.

'They're prisoners,' said Polina.

'These must be the people they take away,' said Mo-Lan. 'They put them to work recording all the debts.' She nodded at a hooded man passing down the centre of the room pushing a trolley. As he walked past the desks, the people writing at them threw in the paper they'd been writing on. Nobody looked up as it happened. It seemed to be something they had done so often that they could now perform the task like machines, never looking up or about or pausing to think or rest.

'He's taking them to wherever they keep the records,' said Victor. 'Let's go after him.'

The hall was as high as a cathedral. The scratching of quills on paper and the sticky snoring of the man with the keys were amplified by the vast emptiness. Every sound echoed endlessly as it bounced between the bare stone walls. Which meant that when Elena decided to call out, her voice filled the entire room.

'Aunty?' she said, hoping to spot her long-lost relative amongst the many thousands of imprisoned clerks.

The keeper of the keys grunted in his sleep. He turned on his stool and his belt of chains clinked ominously.

'Shhh,' said Polina. 'Not yet. If you go looking for her now, it'll cause a commotion and they'll realise we're not real collectors. First we have to destroy the records, then we can turn our minds to freeing the others.'

'How are we going to free them if they're all chained up?' said Elena. 'We can't go around trying to fit ten thousand keys into ten thousand locks.'

'We'll think of something.'

None of them felt good about leaving the hall of villagers behind, frantically scrawling on their sheets of paper by the faint light of flickering candles. But the man pushing the trolley had opened the door at the end of the hall with a heavy key and it seemed as if it might be their one chance to make it into the next chamber.

They rushed along behind him, hoping somehow that he wouldn't notice, and that they'd be able to move along behind him unnoticed.

But he had noticed.

The collector with the trolley turned and stared at them.

'What business have you leaving the Hall of Scribes?' he said, his voice deep and mistrusting.

'We've been called to, uh, the next hall,' said Polina. 'We

don't know why, all we know is we're supposed to head through this door.'

The collector sniffed the air. 'You say you have business with the High Count Bitumen?'

'Yes,' Polina blurted. 'We have business with the High Count.'

'He is expecting you?'

'He is. He'll be furious if you don't take us directly to him.'

'Then come,' said the man. 'I will take you there on my way to the Hall of Records.'

The trolley squeaked like a mouse as it rolled on.

25

The door opened on to a dark stone corridor. It was dimly lit by spluttering candles.

Halfway along, the collector with the trolley turned to a red door in the wall. The door was the shape of a teardrop and decorated with strings of numbers clustered together like stars on a map of the universe. He backed away from it slightly as though afraid of what lay within.

'This is where I leave you,' the collector said. 'That there's the door into the High Count's chamber.'

None of them moved.

'Go in,' he said. 'You'd be well advised not to keep him waiting.'

They all shook with unconcealed fear. Victor could see Polina cursing herself for not having thought quicker. Why couldn't she have said they were supposed to be taken to the Hall of Records? If they went through that door, surely the

High Count would notice that they didn't work for him? And he could only imagine what the collectors might do to them once they'd discovered why they were really there.

'Actually,' said Mo-Lan, 'I'm not one hundred per cent sure we were supposed to see the High Count. Maybe it was something about going to records we were told to do?'

'Yes,' said Mingus, picking up on where she was going. 'I'm fairly sure we're supposed to be going with you to the records room.'

'I see no reason why that would be the case,' said the collector, his eyes narrowing with suspicion. 'No one but me has any business in the hall of records.'

'But I'm sure we were supposed to go with you,' said Victor.

'I believe we've been assigned organising the records,' said Mo-Lan. 'There is supposed to be a new system implemented by which—'

'Enough!' said the collector. 'You are making excuses. Enter now or I will call the guards.'

Polina, her face heavy with guilt and fear, stepped through the door first.

The others followed.

The room they found themselves in was lit by blue orbs that hung from the ceiling.

Sitting on a throne made of twisted glass was a very small man beneath a very large crown. The crown was crafted from sharp, gleaming silver metal, and the man's robe was not black but of the darkest blue. It appeared to be filled with swirling galaxies and milky trails of planets.

'Please,' he said. 'Take off the cloaks. I know you are not of my kind.'

No one moved. Was it a trick? Victor wondered. He felt Saint Oswald's heart speeding up beside his own.

'I said take them off!' boomed the figure, his voice seeming to come from every direction at once. 'You are not fooling anyone. Do you think my guards are so stupid that they could not spot a band of intruders attempting to infiltrate the castle? I know what you are.'

The five of them complied, shaking off their disguises with terror. As Victor lifted away his cloak, he made sure to slip Saint Oswald off at the same time and drop the fabric on the ground in such a way that no one would notice his giant tortoise hiding beneath it.

'If you have come looking for your loved ones, you should have remained with the others in the trees. When you enter here uninvited, you become our property.'

For the first time in the journey, Victor wondered whether he would ever see Rainwater again. He thought of all of the days that had passed by while he dreamt of moving to big cities and wished he could go back and experience them all over again, noticing every little detail, from the way his legs burned as he chased birds off the crops to the feel of the dirt under his fingernails as he tore turnips out of the ground.

'We haven't come looking for anyone,' said Elena, trying to sound much braver than she felt. 'We've come to change things.'

'Is that so?'

The figure stood up. With tiny, trembling arms, he lifted the metal crown from his head and set it down on the chair. He threw back his hood. The man beneath the hood was the oldest person any of the children had ever seen. Patches of wiry hair stuck out of his face at random and large moles and scars mapped his sagging cheeks. The flesh of his head hung from his jaws like the jowls of a dog. He had so much extra skin on his forehead that it folded over his eyes, hiding them almost entirely.

'I have been in this world a great deal longer than any of you,' he said. 'And in that time, I have learned that things never change. They may appear to, but they don't. People, you see, stay the same. They have the same failures and weaknesses as they've always had. How can we expect to build a better world when we do not have better people to build it with?'

'Who are you?' asked Polina.

'They call me the High Count Bitumen,' said the old man. 'The richest man ever to walk upon this land. Though things were not always that way. I was once an exile from the Old West, travelling across the great Eastern Ocean with little more than a battered suitcase and half a dream.'

'You came from the Old West?' she said.

'Indeed,' said the High Count. 'Though not of my own choice. I was sent away, once it was discovered what I had created.'

Polina's mouth fell open in horror. 'You invented the music box. You're the reason they banned inventing.'

'What music box?' said Elena. 'What are you talking about?'

'I told you before,' explained Polina. 'That when I arrived in the Old West, I found that they had banned inventions because someone had created something so awful that it ruined countless lives. This is the man who did it.'

'That's me,' said the old man, reaching into his robe and producing a tiny silver box that was small enough to rest safely on the palm of his hand. 'And this is the very object which had me banished from the place in which I grew up.'

Not having heard stories of its terror, the children weren't particularly shocked by the music box, but Polina moved as far from it as she could, pressing herself against the back wall of the chamber.

'What does it do?' asked Victor.

'Don't go near it,' ordered Polina. 'Get away from it.'

'Just looks like an old music box to me,' said Elena.

'This box,' said the count, 'is capable of playing a song so sad it turns animals to iron and makes the clouds weep.'

'The Iron Plague!' exclaimed Victor. 'You're the one who caused the Iron Plague! You're why all those people and creatures turned to metal!'

The old man's mottled lips twitched. 'So you have heard of my contraption?'

'I've heard of the damage it did,' said Victor. Everything was beginning to make sense to him now. Why Elena hadn't heard of seeds, Mingus didn't know how to make clothes, and Mo-Lan didn't believe you could make glass. 'You used the music box to cause the Iron Plague so that no one could grow or make anything for themselves,' said Victor. 'You made it so that they had to borrow things off you. That way, they were in your debt, and they had to start working to pay you back. You invented the Iron Plague to take control of the kingdom.'

'That's the truth,' said the High Count. 'I am the greatest inventor ever to set foot in this kingdom and I have more power than the king and all his knights put together.'

'But why?' asked Victor. 'Why would you bother? Don't you have all the money you need?'

'It is both very simple and very complicated,' said the High Count. 'I do not expect you to understand.' The old man coughed and spluttered before he could carry on. 'I was born to a poor family,' he said, once he'd regained his composure. 'Very poor. We had less than you could imagine. We grew what we could, made what we could. It was never even close to being enough. Often there were years when we came close to starving because our crop didn't grow and we had nothing to trade. My family lived in constant fear of going without.

'So when I came here, I created a world in which things were simpler. Each village would only have one job to do. One task that they had to work for. This way, they would be free from the worry and uncertainty that my family had suffered from. If they worked hard, they would reap the rewards.'

'You think you're helping us?' asked Mo-Lan in disbelief.

'I am helping you,' said the old man.

'Then why take people away if they can't pay?'

'The larger our operation grows, the more we need people to work here in the fortress. It is for the good of the many that the few must come here. I cannot imagine that you would understand.'

'But why be so cruel? If you're trying to help people, why are you so awful to them?'

'We must protect the system we have built at all costs,' said the High Count. 'Nothing must be allowed to endanger the system. If one person can't pull their weight, they must be cut free, before they pull those around them down.'

'No!' shouted Victor. 'That's not how it works. If one person fails, then the others pick them back up.'

'Do you want to spend your life lifting up the lazy, boy? Do you really want to waste your energy holding up those who cannot be bothered to work, after your families have struggled so hard to keep you afloat?'

Victor balled his fists. There was no way this old man was going to keep him from going back home. He leant over to Elena. 'Distract him,' he whispered.

'But how do you make everything that the villagers need?' Elena asked. 'All of the food and clothes and supplies?'

'Ah, it was only a matter of arranging things to suit us. Quite simple really. I can show you.'

The High Count clicked his fingers and a glass case rose from the stone floor. The glass case was lit from within by a sun the size of an eyeball, perched in one corner.

Inside the case was a model of all the land between the Eastern Ocean and the Saddest Sea. In intricate detail, it showed all the hills and forest, valleys and deserts, villages and cities of the kingdom in which they were standing. Tiny carts were moving around, carrying whatever had been made in one village far across the land.

One village would make bread, and that bread would be distributed to a hundred other villages, while another would make shoes, and those shoes would be distributed to a hundred other villages. In this way, the High Count had ensured that no single village had enough knowledge to prosper on its own. They all relied on his collectors to bring them what they needed.

'You may well be able to spot your homes,' he said. 'Be sure to have a look – it will be the last time you ever see them.'

The three children and Polina shuffled closer to the model while Victor hung back.

As the High Count responded to Elena's questions, Victor crouched and extended his hand to Saint Oswald underneath the table. He passed a match from his pocket into the tortoise's mouth and told her, 'Carry on up the corridor. You saw the way the man with the trolley went. You just need to get into the room with the records and set everything on fire.'

'*Uk, uk,*' whispered Saint Oswald.

'I know, I'm scared too. But you can do it.'

As the count continued to deliver his speech, the giant tortoise crept slowly out of the chamber, the match clutched in her beak.

There was no one to notice her waddle down the corridor.

Or push open the door of the record room.

Or strike the match on her own shell.

'*Uk, uk,*' said Saint Oswald, as the Hall of Records burst into flame.

26

A few moments later, the collector who had been pushing the trolley burst into the count's chamber.

'What is it?' asked the High Count, who had been rather enjoying his opportunity to explain how he had managed to take control of the kingdom.

'Hurry, High Count, the Hall of Records is on fire.'

The old man narrowed his eyes impatiently. 'Is this some sort of joke?

'No, High Count, I'm afraid it isn't.'

The count let out an ear-splitting scream and dashed from the room, forgetting entirely the group of intruders he'd left behind. If the records disappeared, it would be his entire life's work gone, and the system he'd worked so hard to create would come crashing down.

'What now?' said Mingus. 'We still need to free the others and there are all those locks and that big man with the keys and—'

'It is possible,' interrupted Mo-Lan. 'That is, if one of us were to put on his crown, they might believe we were their leader and decide to do what we asked of them.'

They all looked at each other. Victor was too small, Polina was too big, and if either of the two girls attempted to masquerade as the count then their voices would give them away. Only Mingus was the right size and shape to convincingly wear the crown. Polina, Victor, Elena and Mo-Lan turned to face the boy from Aeldbird. Instead of falling to the floor in panic, Mingus slowly nodded.

And swallowed.

And clenched his fists at his sides.

'It has to be me,' he said. 'And I'm a cool, calm lake.'

Elena put a hand on his shoulder and stared him in the eyes.

'Thank you,' she said. 'My aunt is trapped in that room. You'd be saving her.'

Fear flashed across his face. 'W-w-what if I can't do it?'

'You can do it,' said Elena. 'There's just a stupid voice in your head that tells you that you can't do things. The less you listen to it, the more it'll shut up.'

'She's right,' said Mo-Lan. 'It's like Greenbeard taught us: you aren't required to pay attention to all of your unhelpful thoughts.'

Mingus gulped and nodded.

They all helped lift the heavy crown on to his head.

Everyone put their cloaks back on and they trailed along behind Mingus as he tried his best to walk like a hunched old man. It wasn't a hard walk to master, seeing as he was already trembling with fear and walking as slowly as possible toward the first hall.

In the Hall of Scribes, he coughed to get everyone's attention.

No one looked.

'Excuse me,' he muttered.

Still, no one turned around.

'EXCUSE ME!' he roared.

The pens of the clerks stopped their scratching.

The keeper of the keys woke up.

All eyes turned to Mingus.

He shuffled nervously from side to side.

'I am the High Count Bittymon and I demand you release each and every one of these prisoners now,' he said.

'B-b-b-ut why, High Count?' asked the keeper of the keys. 'Who will keep the records? If they stop, we'll fall behind.'

Mingus waved his arms in the air impatiently, finally getting into his role. 'Do you really dare to question me? You lazy idiot. I know you were sleeping this whole time. Now unlock them at once. Or else I'll . . .' He struggled to find a suitable threat. 'Or else I'll feed you to the pigs.'

'Yes, High Count. Of course, High Count.'

As the keeper of the keys set about unlocking the captives, the four children and the inventor fled.

They barrelled out of the gloomy hall, across the courtyard and past the stables where they'd left the horses they'd arrived on.

Seeing their leader approach, the guards on the gates rushed to haul them open.

'Leave these gates open!' shouted Mingus, as they all passed through. 'No matter what anyone tells you, do not close them. By order of me, who is definitely the High Count Bittymon.'

While they'd been inside the dark fortress, the people in the trees had carried their plane to a hiding place near the woods. Greenbeard stood beaming as he watched the four children emerge from the shadow of the castle. Mingus heaved the crown off his head and happily watched it roll away into the undergrowth. Mo-Lan helped him tear the stinking cloak from his shoulders. Together, they hurled it into the air, where it was snatched away by the crow that seemed to follow Greenbeard wherever he went.

Elena ran straight to her uncle. Even for a tree person, he was pale with worry, and he grasped her hands so tightly they turned white.

'Aunty should be coming out of those gates any second,' she said. 'But we have to go. I'll see you back at Moonwald.'

Her uncle planted a joyous kiss on her forehead.

'Go,' he said. 'I'll meet you at home.'

'Hurry,' urged Polina, looking back at the plumes of smoke rising from the fortress. 'We must go as quickly as we can. Once the collectors realise what we've done, they'll come for your villages. They may not be able to take payment, but that doesn't mean they won't want to take revenge. Your parents need to be freed before they reach them. And I do not think we have seen the last of Walter Swizwit.'

The inventor lit the fire below the balloon. The children threw themselves in wherever they could. Victor held Saint Oswald to his chest with clammy hands. Almost as soon as they were above the trees, they could see legions of collectors streaming out of the dark fortress on horseback.

They did not pause to try and keep their prisoners from escaping into the arms of the tree people. Instead they galloped through the trees toward the villages, their horses weaving around trunks and leaping over roots. At the back of his army rode a tiny, ancient man, who had gone a very violent shade of red. He shook his wrinkled fists at the sky in anger.

Coming from the opposite direction, along the main road from Kaftan Minor, rode Walter Swizwit and his army. They were heading for the dark fortress, which now stood empty except for the tongues of flame lashing at its grimy stone walls.

27

The plane thundered through the air, leaving behind a trail of white that cut the sky in two.

Victor longed to go straight home and see his parents, though he knew that was selfish. They all had parents that needed rescuing and it would take all of them working together to make it happen.

He wondered whether his parents would still be in bed. Did they have enough food? And water? How long had he been gone? It couldn't have been more than a week or two, but it felt like whole years had gone by since he'd walked out of Rainwater with Saint Oswald at his side.

What would happen if the dark riders managed to reach the villages before they did? What would they do to the adults who had lost themselves in Polina's inventions? And what would happen when a furious Walter Swizwit eventually caught up with them?

Polina steered the plane down toward the forest. It clipped the crowns of trees as it went.

She flew back and forth a few times over the same spot, until the engine began to grumble about being thirsty and the children started to grow dizzy.

Polina scratched her head in confusion.

'I don't see a village,' she said. 'And these are the co-ordinates you gave me.'

'Are you sure? We learn them when we're young, so that we can find our way home from anywhere in the world,' said Mo-Lan.

Their pilot pointed out a wide, purple island in amongst the endless trees. 'That, apparently, is your village.'

'What is it?'

'I'm not quite sure.'

'Can you land on it?'

'I can try.'

Polina lit the torch that inflated the balloon over the aeroplane. She flew toward the purple island and cut the propeller, leaving them hovering directly over their target. By slowly reducing the size of the flame, she lowered them on to the purple platform.

The children hopped out. They were all relieved to be back on solid ground, even if they weren't exactly sure what the solid ground was made of.

Mo-Lan knelt. She put her nose to the purple island.

She prodded it.

She sniffed it.

She sank her teeth into it.

'We're on the giant turnip!' she said.

'Giant turnip?' asked a confused Polina.

'It's something we had to come up with for the collectors. Without anyone to shave it down, it must have burst through the building and kept growing. Come on, we should be able to slide down the sides if we're careful.'

One by one, they slid down the side of the giant turnip, into Sektun-Layley.

The village was in chaos. Not only had the giant turnip demolished nearby buildings, but every single thing in sight was trussed up with glittering thread. Walking even the shortest distance meant clambering through knots and tangles. Walls had been reduced to rubble, furniture lay in splinters, and shards of glass shone amongst the debris.

'No!' shouted Mo-Lan. 'When the turnip broke through the roof, it must have freed Dr Katz.'

'Dr Katz?' asked Polina.

'Their massive spider,' explained Elena. 'Who spins massive webs.'

'These webs could go on through the entire woods by now. It'll be almost impossible to get through. My parents must be trapped.'

She bounded wildly through the silk threads, tripping and pulling herself back up as she went. Her hair got caught and pulled out. Her knees got skinned and bled.

Mo-Lan found her parents wrapped in cobwebs on the floor of their house, or what was left of it. There was no roof, a single wall, a floor of shiny wooden boards and a coal-burning stove. Broken pieces of the miniature farms were scattered around the ruin. Her parents fought against their bonds when they saw their daughter approaching. A combination of terror and relief blinked across their eyes.

She fell to her knees and started yanking on the thread. It was no good. It was like trying to break chain with your bare hands. The spider's webs were so strong that Mo-Lan struggled to even shift them.

Everyone else caught up with her.

'Get them out,' Mo-Lan pleaded with Polina. 'Please free them; if they stay there much longer then dehydration will begin to set in and they'll become so ill that—'

She tugged on her hair and let loose a scream. 'Those thoughts aren't helping!' Mo-Lan shouted to herself.

'Be a lake,' said Mingus, reaching out to pat his friend between the shoulder blades.

'I'll help them,' Polina said reassuringly.

The inventor dug around in her bag and produced a sharpened diamond that she used to carefully slit the strings that bound Mo-Lan's parents. Once they were free, they buried their daughter in a fierce hug.

'I'm so sorry,' they whispered. 'We don't know what came over us.'

'That's okay,' she told them.

'It's not,' her mother said. 'It was like a spell. Like we had no control, all we wanted to do was play with those tiny farms.'

'They took all of our time and gave us nothing in return,' said her father. 'A little like the collectors in that respect.' He shook his head. 'We almost lost you.'

'No,' said Mo-Lan. 'I almost lost you, but we're all okay.'

The three of them pulled each other into one more hug. Mo-Lan introduced them to her new team of friends and it was left to Polina to give a hurried explanation of everything that had happened.

'You mean we don't owe them anything?' asked Mo-Lan's mum. 'We're free?'

'In a way,' said Mo-Lan. 'But as soon as they realised what

we'd done, they set off for our villages. It can't be long before they arrive.'

'So what now?'

'Now we free everyone else before they get here,' said Mo-Lan.

With the introductions over, everyone set about freeing the trapped scientists and children of Sektun-Layley with diamond cutters. It was hard work. The children soon found their arms aching and their bodies wrapped in silver thread. When they tried to peel it off their clothes, the thread stuck to their hands. When they tried to peel if off their hands, it wound itself around their arms.

'Is that everyone?' Mo-Lan asked eventually. 'I don't think I can carry on.'

'Me neither,' said Mingus. 'My arms are about to fall asleep.'

But they were done.

The newly freed scientists formed a circle in the centre of the village. They sat around a glowing globe that had been invented so that complex experiments could be performed even in the deepest night. The adults were all pink with embarrassment. A number of them carried bright red marks from where the thread had been digging into their skin. The children, on the other hand, looked as though they'd just woken up from month-long naps. They scratched at their tired eyes and let loose wide yawns that bounced between the trees.

'Who wants to go first?' asked one man.

The scientists did not have a mayor or a leader. If a decision had to be made, they would take it in turns to speak and then vote on a course of action. They found things easier that way. Everyone got to talk and everyone got to be listened to, so no one ever felt forgotten.

Mo-Lan's mum was the first to speak.

'Firstly,' she said, 'I would like to thank our daughter and her friends for rescuing us. We lost ourselves for a while but we are back again now, and we have no time to lose.'

People muttered approval.

'But now we face another threat. Though our debts have been erased by the bravery of Mo-Lan and her friends, the collectors will come here to seek revenge. They will want to stop us from spreading word that their records have been destroyed and so they will attempt to destroy us.' She shook her head sadly. 'When our ancestors accepted their offer, all those years ago, we could never have known it would end like this.'

'So what do we do?' someone piped up.

'We leave,' Mo-Lan's father said, looking up. 'What else is

there we can do?' His wife stood and slipped her hand into his. 'We have to run.'

'But they'll follow us,' shouted one man.

'Then let them follow us. We cannot lie down and let ourselves be taken as prisoners. We've already let down our children once – let us not do it again.'

Someone else stood up to talk.

They didn't get chance.

As she opened her mouth to speak, the unmistakable sound of pounding hooves echoed through the town. It was difficult to tell how far away they were but it was clear that they were getting closer. What started as a whispered drumbeat grew steadily into ground-shaking thunder.

'They're already on their way,' said Mo-Lan's mum, dropping her husband's hand and flicking off the giant light that illuminated them all. 'Let's move, quickly. Hopefully the webs will keep them at bay for a while.'

Adults hoisted sleepy children on to their shoulders and, together, they all set off along the forest path. They didn't know how much of the forest the giant spider had strung up or how long it would keep the riders from the black fortress from catching them. Where would they go? How would they start again? Would they ever really be safe from the collectors? They were questions that hurt to think about; it was easier to focus on putting one foot in front of the other.

Mo-Lan, Elena, Mingus, Saint Oswald and Victor walked at the front of the procession, holding torches that cast long shadows on the rough path. Whenever Mingus jumped at the sudden squawks of the night beasts, the giant tortoise would scuttle over and headbutt his ankle reassuringly.

'Do you think they'll catch us?' whispered Mo-Lan.

'Nah,' said Elena.

'Maybe,' said Mingus.

'Not if we stay together,' said Victor. 'They can't take us all on.'

Even though it had been an age since they'd slept, none of the children felt tired. The fear had charged them up. They would see this through to the end, regardless of what the end turned out to be.

28

It was dawn when Aeldbird came into view, though no one would be able to guess that it had once been a village. Every plank of every house had been clawed apart and tossed aside. All that remained were squares of cleared dirt where homes had once stood. In each square of dirt, whole families of hunters sat with their faces pressed into stereoscopes. Their bodies had grown thin and pale and their clothes hung from them in tatters.

The animals circled the distracted hunters, growling and yapping. Strangely, none of them laid a paw on any of the people, though it was clear they were hungry by the great drips of saliva hanging from their mouths.

Polina ordered the procession to a halt a little way outside the village.

'We can't go further as a group,' she said.

'She's right,' said Mo-Lan. 'If we all go in, they'll interpret it as an act of aggression and attack us in response.'

'Exactly,' said Polina.

'Please,' said Mingus. 'Just don't let them eat my parents. They're the only parents I have. They taught me how to use a toilet.'

'We won't let anything happen to them,' said Polina.

'What will you do?' asked Mo-Lan's father.

'I'm going to talk to them. I'm sure they can be reasoned with. They're animals, after all, just like us. They're not rocks or hurricanes.'

'But how are you going to communicate with bears?'

Polina dug around in her suitcase and produced two dented metal helmets, each spilling with wires. A central bundle of wire twisted together in a braid connected the top of one helmet to another. They looked like a giant, overcomplicated version of the tin-can phones Victor had once made so that he could speak with his neighbour on nights when neither of them could sleep.

'These are brain-wave interpreters,' Polina said. 'They'll allow me to understand an animal and that animal to understand me.'

No one was particularly convinced. 'Are you sure?' someone asked.

'I'm positive,' said the inventor. 'I've tried it on three

kinds of fish and a llama. The bears are clearly in charge here, so it's the bears I'll speak to. How different can a bear be to a trout?'

They all watched in terror as Polina put on one of the helmets and marched fearlessly into the centre of the village. She did not appear afraid. She held the spare helmet out ahead of her as though the fearsome bears would know exactly what to do with it.

The animals paused as she approached.

They swung their noses in her direction and sniffed, trying to tell from the air whether she was coming in peace or in war.

Their hackles rose and their mouths twitched.

Polina took another step.

A bunny rabbit hissed.

And another.

The bears reared up, flashing their vicious teeth.

In shock, Polina fell on to her back.

Fear overtook her face. Her plan, it seemed, was not working.

The largest of the bears swiped at her head with its paw. The tips of five claws grazed her forehead. Polina threw her hands up over her head to protect herself.

The villagers of Sektun-Layley wondered whether they

should run in and try to save the inventor. But then wouldn't the bears attack them too? And there was no way they could take on all those beasts. They were scientists, not fighters. They created things; they didn't know how to destroy them.

As the bear moved in to strike another blow, Polina rolled to one side.

The bear crouched to charge.

And Polina leapt into the air, tossing the free helmet as she went. It landed squarely on the bear's head. With a swift movement, she flicked a switch which sent a blue crackle of electricity shooting through the braid of wires connecting the helmets.

The bear's eyes narrowed.

It yowled something at the other bears, who all backed away in confusion. It was clear that Polina had managed to put her device on to whoever was in charge.

The bear wearing the helmet became far calmer than it had been. It tilted its head to one side, intent on listening to something inside the helmet. Then it dropped itself on to the ground. The bear sat on its back two legs like a human, folding its front two in its lap.

Polina sat opposite the bear.

The villagers were too far away to hear what was going on, though it was clear a negotiation was taking place.

Polina would raise her hand
and the bear would nod. The
bear would shake its head
and Polina would shrug.
For fifteen minutes, the
inventor and the bear
spoke through the
helmets.

  Soon enough,
the bear plucked
the helmet off
its head and
tossed it to

one side. Polina picked it up and carried it back to the
waiting group of people.

  'What's going on?' everyone wanted to know.

'He says they're waiting for the king of the bears to emerge from hibernation. That's the only reason they haven't eaten them yet. Once the king comes out, he'll give them orders about what to do with the hunters.'

'What does he think the king of the bears will say?' asked Elena.

'That it's okay to eat them.'

'No!' shouted Mingus. 'You can't let them eat my village.'

'I've made a deal,' Polina explained. 'If we let them take all of the cages and promise never to hunt any of the animals again, they'll leave.'

'But we're a hunting village,' pleaded Mingus. 'It's all we know how to do.'

'Would you rather be an eaten village?'

Mingus shook his head, tears in his eyes.

Mo-Lan wrapped her arms around him and squeezed. 'It'll be okay,' she whispered. 'You won't have to hunt any more because you won't owe anything to the collectors, remember?' Mingus sniffled. 'What are you?' she asked him.

'I'm a cool, calm lake,' replied Mingus, his eyes puffy with tears.

Polina coughed to catch the attention of the group.

'The bears have also agreed to head off the way we came,' she said. 'That way, they'll force the collectors back. They may be determined but I doubt they'll want to face down an army of wild animals. I should imagine they'll try to loop round the woods and meet us later on. By then, we may have come to the last of your villages.'

'And then what?'

'And then we'll see.'

In the long, low storage shed, Mingus sullenly unhooked the cages and nets used to hunt animals. Although he had never liked hunting, he knew that the tools were invaluable to his parents. All they knew how to do was hunt, and without their equipment, they'd never be able to do it again.

Once he was done, he stepped back.

'Go on,' he said to the waiting mass of creatures. 'You can take them.'

And so all of the bears and rabbits and squirrels and weasels carried away the cages that had trapped their brothers and sisters, leaving behind a town of people sitting on bare ground with stereoscopes pressed firmly to their faces.

'Now what do we do?' asked Mingus, blowing his nose. 'They're still watching those stupid things.

Polina pulled a set of slides from her bag and passed them out to everyone. 'Drop these into the stereoscopes,' she told them. 'So far, they've been watching a happy family splash at the beach, play games and eat beautiful meals, but this is only one part of their lives. It is a trick. You could make a jail cell look beautiful, if you only showed the view from its window. These extra slides, they will show the less shiny parts of the family's life: the arguments, the shouting, the loneliness, the growing up and moving apart.'

'But who are the family?' asked Victor.

Polina shrugged. 'I made them up.'

'Why would you do that?'

The inventor thought. 'I suppose,' she said, 'that I wanted to make what I'd never had. More than anything, it was a fantasy. I never had a perfect family and so I wanted to create a way of spending time with one. There are two things wrong with that. The first being that you are not really spending time with anyone, you only feel as though you are. And the second being that there is no such thing as a perfect family, so every family that appears to be so must be an illusion. You cannot have the light without the dark, or you would see nothing.'

She shook her head, bringing herself back to the present moment. 'Everyone take a few and slot them into the stereoscopes. Be warned,' she said. 'Your parents might be a little fragile once they come back to us. They've been lost in the lives of these people for a good long while now.'

The villagers of Sektun-Layley darted through the ruins of Aeldbird, dropping the new slides into the stereoscopes.

Once they were done, everyone gathered in the centre of the town to see whether or not the inventor's plan would work.

'How long will it take?' Mingus asked.

'I'm not sure,' replied Polina.

One by one, the hunters of Aeldbird lifted their eyes from the stereoscopes. The eyes were shadowed by tiredness and many were glinting with tears. They were the eyes of people saying goodbye.

When Mingus's parents finally lowered their devices, he rushed toward them.

They bumped noses.

They growled.

(This was the way the hunters of Aeldbird greeted each other. Nobody could remember why. Mingus guessed it was because the old people had such bad breath that none of them wanted to kiss each other.)

'They almost ate you!' he exclaimed, firing a gentle punch into his dad's arm.

'Who did?' his dad asked blearily.

'The bears,' said Mingus, gesturing at the flattened village. 'Look, they tore down our houses and took our cages and now they've gone.'

His parents stared miserably out at the remnants of Aeldbird.

'They took our cages?'

Wiping his nose, Mingus nodded. 'I'm sorry. We didn't have a choice. We had to give them everything so they wouldn't eat you. We also had to promise we wouldn't hunt them ever again.'

'Never hunt again?' said his father. 'Nonsense. What'll we do if we don't hunt?'

'Manage is what we'll do,' said Mingus's mother. 'We got ourselves into this mess; now we ought to get ourselves right out of it.'

As the rest of the Aeldbird hunters realised that all of their stores had been emptied, panic set in. Even after Victor had explained that the collectors no longer had records of what they owed, the hunters couldn't settle down. There was talk of fighting, of setting up guard-towers and walls and arming themselves with improvised weapons.

But the fighting talk was empty.

No one would dare stand up to the collectors. At least not in a fight. Over the years, they had made so much money that going against them was impossible. They had turned themselves into the largest, fastest and best-equipped army in the kingdom. Their numbers dwarfed even those of King Marshalla's forces.

Not knowing what else to do, Victor, Elena and Mo-Lan

filled a giant pot with water and set it on a fire to boil. They worked together to create a tea that was a mixture of camomile, ginger and lavender. It was a tea designed to calm the nerves and slow down a racing brain.

They dashed between the destroyed houses, passing out cups to the hunters.

The moon rose.

And the hunters began to settle.

They fell into hushed chats with the scientists of Sektun-Layley, comparing stories of the pedlar who had rolled into town and tricked them all into buying such useless inventions. They all agreed that it had felt like falling under a strong magic. The lure of the creations had been so powerful that they had forgotten themselves entirely. Most of the adults could barely remember the time that had passed since the pedlar's arrival. It was as though someone had snatched the time between then and now and thrown it away.

And now they were faced with the might of the collectors, furious at having been outwitted. And Walter Swizwit, with his own army and the fury of someone who was close to losing everything.

It was not long before hoofbeats echoed through the forest.

The collectors had managed to find a way through the

spider's web. They were heading toward the next village. Though animals would chase them off the path, it wouldn't be long before they found another route toward the fleeing villagers. There was no time to lose. Bags were packed and the rubble was searched for anything useful.

Once again, it was decided that there was nothing to do but press on. Everyone agreed to venture forward to Moonwald and help the inhabitants there to free themselves of the inventions that had imprisoned them.

29

Between Aeldbird and Moonwald, the woods were at their thickest. The large group of villagers tramped along the path. Most of them were exhausted. They breathed heavily and took it in turns carrying each other. As they went, birds rushed from the trees and rodents scurried into their dens.

It soon became clear that the group would need to take a break for sleep before they managed to reach Moonwald. As a precaution, they left the path and wandered deeper into the forest. They stopped in a clearing hemmed with polka-dot mushrooms.

'Should we go further?' asked one scientist.

A vote was held and it was decided that they shouldn't. If they walked any further, they might not find their way back.

Camp was quickly built from whatever materials were to hand. Parents arranged rags into beds for their children.

Dead branches were propped against trees for shelter. Victor, Elena, Mingus, Mo-Lan and Saint Oswald all crowded together under a single sheet strung between trees, using their remaining squares of cloth as blankets. They had one candle stub between them. They used it to light up the canvas ceiling and they made their hands into shapes that danced as shadow puppets overhead.

The least-tired adults were given mugs of strong tea and made to take the first watch. They sat at the edges of the camp, lit torches trapped between their legs. To keep awake they practised birdcalls and made pebbles appear and disappear from their palms. The blackness was so thick that the guards relied more on their ears than their eyes to warn them of any incoming danger. Unexpected creaks and rustles had them leaping to their feet, only to sit back down again once they'd convinced themselves the sounds were innocent.

'What was that?' whispered Mingus in the makeshift tent.

'What was what?' asked Victor.

'That sound.'

'I think it was Saint Oswald.'

'Nah,' said Elena. 'It was me.'

'What was you?'

'Shh,' whispered Mo-Lan. 'Some of us are trying to sleep.'

'You shhh,' whispered Elena. 'Some of us are trying to talk.'

'Shhh yourself.'

'Shhh.'

'Shhhhh.'

'Shhhhhhh.'

And they all shhhed each other until they giggled and started slipping into sleep, falling silent one by one.

Sleep was hardly less busy than the waking world. Their dreams were raucous. There are some people who, when the world becomes a dangerous and scary place, fall asleep and dream dangerous and scary dreams. There are other people who have their most beautiful, peaceful dreams when the waking world is heaving with terrible things. Of the four children, only Elena was this second type of person. She dreamed she was on a floating bed, drifting peacefully down a glassy river alongside bright petals and chirping dolphins.

At the edge of the camp, one of the guards got up from where he was sitting. He could have sworn he'd seen something, something bigger than a squirrel or an owl. Were there blue tigers this side of the ocean? Apes? Wild dogs?

He squinted.

Was someone there?

'Hello?' he called out.

And then he saw it.

The horse and its rider had positioned themselves behind

a spindly tree and were standing so still it was hard to believe they were alive. Though they were difficult to make out clearly, he could see the folds of a cloak and the tired whites of the horse's eyes.

Knowing that if he didn't act straight away, the collector would get away and give the rest of his crew their location, the guard ran as fast as he could toward the intruder.

'Halt!' shouted the man on the horse.

But the guard did not.

With a sharp kick in the ribs, the man on the horse spurred his steed on. They shot away from their hiding place. In seconds, the intruders were nearly out of sight, obscured by the foliage and the lifting night.

The guard tore the bow from his back, fitted an arrow into it and let it fly. His aim was perfect. He caught the cloak of the rider, pinning him to a nearby tree as his horse galloped away from under him.

The collector screamed to be let down. He unleashed a torrent of angry threats. 'You've made a terrible choice!' he promised. 'They'll break every bone in your body!'

The guard didn't even pause to reply.

It would take the man a while to get down from the tree, but it would be no time at all before the horse had reached the other collectors and led them to the villagers.

Back at the camp, the guard marched in circles, shouting and clanging pots to wake the sleeping villagers.

'We've been found!' he bellowed. 'Time to move! Collectors coming!'

Tents were left up.

Fires were left burning.

Everyone rushed back on to the path and began trooping toward Moonwald. They went half-dressed, with hair in messy nests and the crumbs of sleep still sticking to their eyes. They held each other by the hands and prayed silent prayers for a miracle to save them.

30

Woken up by all the noise, the children of Moonwald were already waiting in the middle of their village when everyone arrived. They stood blinking in the light of the moon, mucky faces dark around the whites of their eyes. They raised their hands and waved. Everyone else waved back.

'Have you come to help us?' asked one of the children.

'We hope so,' answered Polina.

After working so hard for so long, the children had fallen asleep and slept for three days and three nights. They had woken up and realised that they were so far behind with collecting the rubies, there was no way they'd have enough by the time the collectors came. They hadn't gone back into the mine after that. They'd spent the days scavenging for roots and berries and trying (unsuccessfully) to pull their parents away from the mirrors.

Elena hugged her friends. They explained to her that nothing had changed and the adults were still sitting motionless in their homes, staring into the mirrors. She told them that they were being pursued by the collectors, but that if they managed to get away, they'd never have to work in the mines again. She also told them that they'd come with the real inventor and that she was going to help fix their parents.

'Quickly,' said Elena to Polina. 'You need to wake the adults up before the collectors get here.'

'Don't worry,' said the inventor. 'This one won't be so difficult.'

She sank a hand into her bag and came out with a small, bird-shaped whistle made of glass. Closing her eyes, Polina blew into it. The note that came from the instrument was far too high to be heard by human ears. It cut silently through the air.

Instead of the note, the children heard:

tsk

tsk

tsk

as mirrors throughout the village of Moonwald shattered into thousands of pieces.

The adults who had been staring into them were distraught. Rather than snapping out of their daze, they panicked. They ran out of their houses, waving the broken shards of mirror. They could no longer see themselves and this had their hearts going double-time. 'What if we have spots?' they muttered. 'What if we're dirty or sweaty or our hair is out of place? We must see ourselves! We have to know!'

Just then, all of them seemed to have the same idea at the same time.

Instead of going to greet the villagers who had come to rescue them, they made for the stream that separated their village from the dark forest encircling it.

Polina's face fell. She cursed herself. It didn't make any sense. With the mirrors gone, the people were supposed to have gone back to how they'd been before. Were they really beyond rescue? Was this all her fault? Had they been looking at themselves for too long to go back to looking at the world?

'No!' shouted Elena at her parents. 'You idiots! There's no time! What's wrong with you? Can't you hear them coming?' She turned to Polina. 'Help them,' she said. 'Do something. You said you could help them.'

As Elena despaired, the villagers of Moonwald were peering into their stream. They could remember that water would show them their reflections too, not as well as the mirrors had, but it would be good enough for now.

And for a while, they saw their own faces and sank back into a trance. They brushed stray hairs out of their eyes and combed their eyebrows and rubbed smudges of dirt off their cheeks. Only once they were convinced that they looked perfect could they relax. They smiled empty smiles as they watched their own clean faces staring back at them.

And then they saw the moon in the water, bright and perfect in the mirrored sky.

'Look,' said Elena's mother, pointing. 'It's beautiful.'

The miners of Moonwald tore their eyes away from their own reflections, tipped back their heads and watched the moon where it hung like a pearl in the sky. They felt their hearts slap their ribs. Here was the moon, the ten-thousand-mile-away moon, the same moon that had watched over their planet for millions of years, the moon that wolves howled at and sailors navigated by and children spoke to as if it was a long-lost friend. Here was the moon, and if they wanted it, all they had to do was tilt their heads back and open their eyes.

The spell was broken.

And the Moonwalders were themselves again.

Elena's parents went to her and lifted her off the ground. Elena cried out in surprise. She pummelled them with headbutts. 'How dare you?' she said. 'How dare you forget about me? How dare you forget about everything but yourselves?'

'We know,' said her mother. 'We know.'

'Nah,' said Elena. 'You don't know. You don't know anything.'

'We're so sorry, poppet,' said her father.

'Well, you should be. Everything's fallen apart since you've been gone.'

But their reunion was cut short.

Eyes had appeared between the trees that surrounded Moonwald. Clouds of breath unfurled from the nostrils of horses. On their backs, the shadowy shapes of riders loomed. They had the village surrounded and there was nowhere to run.

31

Everyone in the village of Moonwald froze: the miners, just out of their trances, the hunters, hands jumping to weapons, and the scientists, their eyes closed shut as they tried to think their way out of a situation that felt impossible to escape.

Nobody knew what to do.

Except for Elena.

'Everyone!' she shouted. 'Into the mine!'

Not having any other plan, everyone rushed to follow her order. They sprinted into the darkness, helping each onward. The mineshaft turned a corner a few minutes into the cliff-face, which meant that after only a few steps you were plunged into near-total darkness. The people ran with their hands flat on the walls, trying to keep themselves from crashing into rock.

They stumbled over each other. They tripped and fell.

They helped each other up and carried on.

Mo-Lan ran in, holding the hands of her parents.

Mingus rode in on the shoulders of his dad.

Elena told her parents to go on without her.

'What for?' they wanted to know, not wanting to leave their daughter behind.

'Just go,' she said, shoving them between the shoulder blades. 'You've already caused enough trouble.'

Soon, almost everyone had rounded the turn in the mine and disappeared into its depths.

The collectors had come forward out of the trees. They were leading their horses calmly through the stream, hooves splashing in clear water. Clearly, they weren't in a hurry. The villagers would not be able to outrun them. And by retreating into the mine, they'd only trapped themselves.

Elena grabbed Victor and held him back as everyone else filed into the gloom. 'Do you have any more tortoise poo?' she asked him.

He did. Saint Oswald had only just done one earlier that day and, remembering his mother's words, Victor had been carrying it in a bag ever since. He passed it over and Elena emptied it on to the ground.

'Help me,' she said.

Together they threw handfuls of the poo at the ceiling of

the mine. When enough of it had stuck to the rock, Elena picked a hefty rock off the ground, took off her sock and put the rock into the sock.

'What are you doing?' Victor asked.

'You'll see.'

She took a box of matches out of her pocket.

'Wait,' said Victor. 'Is this safe?'

'Nah,' said Elena. 'But neither is anything else.'

And she struck the match, lit her rock-in-a-sock, and hurled it at the ceiling.

The burning missile ignited the tortoise poo with a whoosh.

The sound of the explosion echoed like thunder around them.

And the ceiling of the mine crumbled, falling in boulders that piled up until the last specks of moonlight disappeared from view.

The villagers had been sealed in; the collectors had been sealed out.

32

They caught up with everyone else deeper in the mine. Although the people of Moonwald had been plucking rubies from its walls for centuries, no one knew how far the mine went or if it led anywhere. They had not dug the mine. It had existed since their grandmothers' grandmothers were babies. Ancient tales claimed that it had been the work of a shy god, who decided to make a quiet place for himself away from the rest of the world. In the stories, the god lived alone for many years, until a lost girl stumbled into his hiding place. The quiet god was so panicked that he exploded into a million rubies.

'Now what do we do?' one of the miners said in the darkness.

'What do you think we do?' a scientist replied. 'We keep going.'

'But you don't know where this thing leads,' protested

one of the hunters.

'It has to lead somewhere.'

'It's a mine, not a tunnel. Why does it have to lead somewhere?'

Elena faked a cough. 'The entrance is all sealed up,' she said. 'And arguing isn't going to save us. So let's just hope it does lead somewhere.'

The arguing stopped and the great walk began.

In the endless dark, it was impossible to tell whether it was morning, noon or night. To save the few matches and torches the group had, they held hands and formed a giant chain that shuffled deeper and deeper into the cave.

When they lit matches, the stone walls around them glimmered with the red of a thousand rubies.

When they didn't, the darkness covered everything.

There were occasional bursts of screaming and screeching when bats left their corners and swooped low over the procession. Sometimes, deep puddles were encountered, and the tallest villagers would have to ferry everyone else across. Other times, bottomless holes appeared in the rock under their feet, and people had to either leap or be thrown across.

Younger kids rode on the shoulders of their parents and older kids took turns carrying the babies of their families.

They all trudged along.

Victor's heart was heaviest. At least Mo-Lan, Mingus and Elena had been reunited with their parents; at least they'd gotten a chance to see their villages one last time. Everyone he knew was still stuck in bed, writhing in pain with whatever illness the pedlar had inflicted on them. Polina probably wouldn't be able to help them anyway, he told himself. She'd barely been able to help Elena's parents. If the moon hadn't been there when they needed it, the Moonwalders would still be staring at their own reflections, and the collectors would have already hauled them away.

As if they could read his mind, Victor's three friends and his giant tortoise appeared at either side of him.

'We might still get there,' said Mo-Lan reassuringly.

'How?' asked Victor.

'We don't know where the mine leads, therefore it could lead to your home.'

'Maybe it leads to a city,' said Mingus. 'A massive one where everyone still goes around in the streets eating bread and laughing and singing songs about happy monkeys.'

'Could lead nowhere,' said Mo-Lan. 'Mines don't normally lead anywhere, they only lead to the substance that is being mined.'

'But where else are we going to go!' said Victor.

'Nowhere,' said Elena. 'So come on.'

They stopped speaking after that. It didn't feel like there was much else to say.

Eventually the silence was broken by someone else.

'Stop!' called a voice from up ahead.

It was one of the Moonwald miners who'd been leading the procession. He'd collided with rock, lit a torch, and found that they were at a crossroads. 'Here,' he said. 'Looks like we have some serious thinking to do.'

Rather than two directions, the mine split into ten separate tunnels, each of which looked identical to the ones beside it. From where the villagers were standing, the only options were ten equally black circles of emptiness. Upset mumbles broke out amongst the people.

The only clue as to which way they ought to take was a brief riddle cut into the stone ceiling of the mine. The words were faint and difficult to make out. A torch was lit and held up to illuminate it.

THREE WAYS TO PEACE
AND TWO TO WAR.
FIVE WAYS LEAD NOWHERE
ANY MORE.

Unable to make any sense of it, the people sent out scouts to check where each of the tunnels ended up. When the scouts returned, they explained that each passage came to a point where it divided up into ten more passages, and that those ten passages each eventually divided up into ten more passages too.

No one could agree on what to do.

A number of the villagers thought they should simply wait until the collectors had gone and then dig their way out of the entrance. Others thought they needed to press on, but as no one could agree on which route to take, it was decided that they would stay put for the time being. There was no point in making a rushed decision. A few people still had packs filled with rations and flasks topped up with water.

Biscuits were broken in half and shared out. Flakes of dried meat were rationed, along with portions of rice and dried flowers.

Everyone took it in turns staring at the riddle.

The scientists of Sektun-Layley stared the longest. Most of them were certain that if they thought hard enough, they'd be able to find some hidden meaning in it and choose a path that led to safety.

'What do you think it means?' whispered Victor in the corner where they'd all tried to make themselves comfortable.

'I think it means that we're never getting out of here,' said Elena, not bothering to keep her voice low.

'You don't think that,' Victor.

She sighed. 'I don't know what I think, except that I wish I was at home and I hate that stupid pedlar and I wish we hadn't even burned the stupid records.'

'You do?' asked Victor. 'If we hadn't, you'd have to spend your whole life mining rubies.'

'Oh, what do you care?' said Elena. 'Apparently you come from a perfect village where the sun always shines and everyone just wanders around doing whatever they want!'

Victor felt close to tears. 'I never said that,' he stuttered. 'I just said we made things for ourselves.'

Elena crossed her arms. 'Good for you.'

'I tried to help you!' said Victor. 'I could have just asked Polina to fix everyone at home but I came with you to the dark fortress because I wanted to help your village and Mingus's and Mo-Lan's!'

'What do you want, a medal?' Elena crouched, picked a glimmering stone off the floor and tossed it at Victor's chest. 'Have a ruby for your trouble.'

With that, Elena sulked off to a dark corner and lay down. Trembling, Victor curled up beside Saint Oswald.

'*Uk*,' said the tortoise.

Victor didn't respond.

They were down to only a few matches. When the last of the torches went out, they weren't relit. In darkness, the village-less villagers slept.

33

It was Elena who woke up first. She opened one eye and saw a white light passing by. Stretching her arms wide and yawning, she sat up.

Her first thought was that she was dreaming, though a few firm pinches put a stop to that.

The mine was alight with glowing ghosts, floating serenely over the sleeping villagers. The ghosts were nodding at each other, smiling and gossiping in whispers. They were all dressed in old-fashioned clothes. Their overalls had old brass buttons down the fronts and they wore cloth caps rather than protective helmets. Some of the ghosts had great white scars across their faces; others were missing fingers, ears or eyes.

Elena wasn't sure how to speak to ghosts.

She cleared her throat.

'Hello?' she said.

Most of the ghosts ignored her, though one swooped down low and came to a halt directly in front of where she was sitting.

'You have the family nose,' the ghost said, smiling kindly. 'Heaven knows where those eyes came from.'

Family nose? thought Elena. She squinted, trying to make out the phantom's face. And she realised the ghost looked like her mum, only older, far older.

'Who are you?' Elena asked.

'I'm Ellantine,' said the woman. 'Your great-great-great-grandmother. Although I was once a girl too.'

'Am I making you up?'

'That's not for me to answer.'

Elena closed her eyes for five seconds and then opened them again. Nothing had changed. Ghosts still filled the mine. Her heart still galloped in her chest.

'Do you live here?' Elena asked the ghost of her great-great-great-grandmother.

The ghost laughed. 'No more than you do,' she said. 'We're only memories. We spent so long down these mines that we all ended up leaving parts of ourselves here. Rubies are wonderfully good at holding on to memories. You should try telling something to one; it'll never forget.'

*

That was the moment that Victor woke up. His first instinct was to scream but something told him that was a bad idea, and instead he shoved a fist into his mouth and bit down on it. Elena noticed him. She put her hands out reassuringly.

'You don't have to be scared,' she said. 'At least I don't think so.'

'Are they ghosts?' Victor whispered, pointing at the swirling mass of silver folk overhead.

'They say they're memories. This is my great-great-great-grandmother.'

'Pleased to meet you,' said Ellantine. 'I would shake your hand, but I doubt you'd feel it.'

'Can you help us get out of here?' Victor wanted to know.

'We can,' the ghost said. 'I'm only sorry we led you here in the first place.'

'How is it your fault?'

'It was us who signed the deal. Many years ago, when the riders turned up in the very mine in which you're both sitting.'

'You made the deal with the collectors?'

'They were dark days,' said Ellantine. 'Every leaf, flower, bird and bug had turned to iron, and the skies had split open and been pouring for forty days. All of the villages in the forest held a meeting and we realised there was nothing we could do but wait out the storm and hope that new life began to grow. So all of us trekked deep into this mine with the last of our supplies and prepared to wait out the Iron Plague.

'For twenty days and twenty nights, we slept where you sleep now. All of us were starving and freezing. No one dared move. Except for one woman, one strange, brave woman, called the Great-Great Grandmother, who led those who would follow her even deeper into these mines. And we never saw them again.'

'Wait,' said Victor. 'The Great Aunt in my village told me about her! She said the Great-Great Grandmother led people to our valley and started Rainwater during the Iron Plague.'

'Then you have been one of the lucky ones,' said Ellantine. 'You have your ancestors to thank for their courage.'

'Does that mean Rainwater is at the end of one of these paths?'

'It must do.'

Victor felt so relieved he thought he might pass out.

'But then what happened to you?' asked Elena. 'When the others left, what did you do?'

'Eventually the collectors rode in on their horses. They had huge amounts of food with them and they told us we could eat as much as we wanted, and that they would bring us more, but we would have to remain here and mine rubies, and the others would have to go with them and be given tasks in other parts of the forest.

'So we accepted their tools and got to work, thinking that we would soon be back to normal. But while we were working in here, we couldn't gather food or make anything for ourselves any more. We were forced to accept all of those things from the collectors. That put us in even deeper into their debt.

'Each month, they came to collect rubies.

'We could never pay them back. Every year, we owed them more. Our children grew up in homes owned by the collectors, eating food provided by the collectors, off plates that belonged to the collectors. They worked in the mines, gathering rubies to give to the collectors, just like their children would have to do.'

'They tricked you!' Elena blurted out. 'They caused the Iron Plague so they could take control of everything!'

'Perhaps they did, perhaps they didn't, perhaps we should have walked away when we still had the chance, instead of living out our lives in service to people who cared nothing about us.'

'Don't say that,' said Elena. 'It isn't your fault. You were only trying to make things better.'

'But we failed, didn't we?'

The ghost of Ellantine moved her face very close to Elena's.

They both blinked.

Ellantine smiled, a sad smile, with entire years hidden inside it.

'Don't lose sight of your life,' she whispered. 'It's this, what you have right now, not some imaginary thing that'll appear one day in the future.'

'I'll try.'

'You try, dear. You try.'

And with that, Ellantine faded into nothing.

The ghosts behind her dissolved too, disappearing into the dark rock of the deep cave.

The two children sat in stunned silence.

Around them, the villagers snored and fidgeted in their sleep.

Victor used the last of their matches to light a lantern. 'Do you think they were really there?' he said, pawing at the empty air.

'They looked real,' said Elena. 'Victor?'

'Yes?'

'I'm sorry for shouting at you. I know we're going to find your village and I'm going to love it. Thank you for coming with us into the dark fortress even though you didn't have to and thank you for taking me with you when you came through Moonwald.'

'Thank you for coming with me too,' said Victor.

She sighed. 'I don't think I really liked the city.'

'I don't think I liked it either. Maybe it was exciting once, but now it's just sad. What do we need a city for anyway?'

'*Uk, uk,*' said Saint Oswald, who was annoyed to have been woken from a rather pleasant dream involving a juicy tomato so big she bit her way in and turned it into a house.

At the sound of the talking, Mo-Lan and Mingus blinked awake and yawned, stretching their arms wide.

'What's going on?' asked Mingus. 'Has something happened?' He frowned. 'Something always happens when I fall asleep.'

'Nah,' said Elena. 'We're just talking about what we're going to do when we get to Victor's village. I told him he'll have to let us all live in his house until we build our own.'

'Can I sleep under your bed?' asked Mingus.

Victor wrinkled his nose. 'Under it?'

'I prefer small, dark spaces. They're cosier. At home, I usually sleep in the cupboards. Mum and Dad say I should have been born a jar of pickles.'

Victor laughed. 'You can sleep under the bed if you want – it might not be that comfortable.'

'Where will I sleep?' asked Elena.

'You can sleep on top of the bed. I'll go in the hammock; I prefer it anyway because it makes me dream of being on the ocean. Mo-Lan can go—'

'Hey,' said Mo-Lan, interrupting them. 'Look.'

She pointed up at the riddle cut into the rock. Below the original four lines, a further four had appeared:

THE WORLD ISN'T FLAT,
FEW BOGBIRDS ARE THIS,
SINCE THE IRON PLAGUE FELL,
THE WORLD'S BEEN AMISS.

'What does that mean?' said Mingus.

'No idea,' said Victor. 'That the world isn't flat?'

'But how is that supposed to help us get out?'

Elena turned to Mo-Lan. 'Do you think you can answer it?'

The girl from Sektun-Layley tilted her head and stared at the riddle. She mouthed the words. 'Give me a second,' she said.

She sat down and crossed her legs, just as Greenbeard had taught her, back when they'd been staying with the tree people. Thoughts darted in and out of her mind like fish. A thousand and one answers formed and burst behind her eyes.

'I don't have to stop thinking entirely,' she told herself in a whisper. 'I just have to learn to control my thoughts, like Mingus did back at the fortress. Don't let them run away.'

For five minutes, she sat perfectly still, hands in her lap. Every now and again, one of her fingers would twitch, as though it wanted to reach for her hair, but Mo-Lan would prevent it from reaching up.

'I've got it,' she said, eventually, her eyes snapping open. 'The world isn't flat, that's right. Bogbirds are nearly extinct on this side of the ocean, so few of them are left. And things have been wrong since the Iron Plague. So we take the right tunnel then the left then the right again. It's simple really.'

'You're a genius!' proclaimed Mingus, enveloping Mo-Lan in a hug.

'That was amazing,' admitted Elena.

Together they woke the rest of the sleeping villagers. No one could understand where the extra lines had come from. Most people guessed that they must have been hidden by a layer of dust that had been blown off. They didn't care; they had a way out.

34

Now that they knew they were on the right track, no one wanted to waste any time. The last matches were used to light the last torches and every man, woman and child got to their feet and started shuffling down the right-hand tunnel.

There was an energy in the air.

People swung their arms as they walked and wondered aloud about where they were going.

Victor ran on ahead of the group. He'd been given a torch to carry and moved so fast that its flame dragged in the air. In his head, he saw his parents. He imagined great things and he imagined terrible things. He imagined his village how he'd left it and his village destroyed the way that Moonwald, Aeldbird and Sektun-Layley all had been.

He ran.

And ran.

And ran.

Until his lungs throbbed and his feet burned.

And then he saw it.

The opening that appeared was criss-crossed by spindly branches. Through them, Victor glimpsed stars. He felt his heart fly up into his head.

'We're here!' he screamed back. 'We're at the end.'

He didn't wait for the others to catch up.

Furiously, Victor tore at the branches until his hands bled. The opening was only about the size of a plate. First, he lifted Saint Oswald through, then he barrelled ahead and forced himself through the gap.

Victor gasped.

He'd emerged at the foot of the smallest mountain that stood beside the village of Rainwater.

The ghosts had sent them back where they belonged.

'We're home,' said Victor to his tortoise.

'*Uk, uk,*' said Saint Oswald.

'It even smells the same.'

'*Uk, uk,*' said Saint Oswald.

'You're right,' said Victor. 'And like porridge and dark chocolate too.'

Not wanting to waste any more time, Victor pelted toward his house with the tortoise under his arm. He passed all the familiar landmarks of his village: the cow sheds, the wheat fields, the tree that he'd once fallen out of and broken his foot. Everything was how it ought to be, painted with a lick of moonlight and watched over by an endless ocean of stars.

Feet kicking up dirt, he legged it across the village green.

And there was his house, too.

Just as he'd left it.

Inside, he found his parents still in their bed. They were thin, pale and more wrinkled than when he'd left them. They looked exhausted, like they'd barely slept a wink the whole time he'd been gone. But they were his parents and they were there.

He threw himself on them in a hug.

For the first time, he felt bigger and heavier than the people who'd made him, and the feeling confused him.

'Victor?' his mum asked, forcing open her eyes. She looked awful, they both did, but there was a spark in their eyes that Victor had never seen before. Was he imagining it, or did they almost look happy?

'It's him!' shouted his dad. 'Our son has returned! Of course he's returned!'

'Are you two okay? Did you have enough food? And water?'

'We're okay, son. We're okay.'

'Did you bring help?' asked his mum. 'Did you get a cure from that evil man?'

'I've got someone that's going to fix everything,' Victor promised. 'Just wait there.'

'We're not going anywhere.'

Victor went to leave.

'Victor!' bellowed his dad, as Victor was almost out of the door.

'Yes, Dad?'

'We've missed you, son.'

'I've missed you too.'

'Good! Now leave that tortoise with us, it feels like an age since we've seen him.'

'Actually,' said Victor, 'he's a she. Polina told me. You can tell by the shape of the shell.'

Victor's dad chuckled and shook his head. 'Well, I've learned something new, haven't I?'

Running back the way he'd come, Victor came to the villagers crawling out of the mine. They were blinking as their eyes adjusted to the bright light of the moon and stars. Some of them lay down to feel the grass against their faces. Others sank their hands into the soil.

Victor tugged at Polina's shirt. He tugged the inventor all

the way back to his house. Once they'd gotten there, Polina took one look at the sick parents and asked to speak to Victor in the kitchen.

'What is it?' Victor asked. 'Can you help them?'

'Of course I can,' said Polina. 'I created the powder that made this all happen.'

Victor scrunched up his face. 'Why would you make something like that?'

'It was a terrible, evil invention,' said Polina. 'I came upon it entirely by accident. And I know I should have gotten rid of it, but the results were too interesting.'

'How is it interesting? It's horrible. You've made everyone sick to their stomachs.'

'What's interesting about it is that your parents aren't sick at all,' explained the inventor.

'Of course they are!' protested Victor. 'They've been in bed for weeks – they can hardly move!'

'The trick of the powder is to plant the idea of illness inside people. There are sicknesses that come to us from the world, and there are those that we grow inside ourselves. Each is as serious as the other but their cures are different.

'If I told you that you were sick, you would tell me I was wrong. But you wouldn't be able to shake the idea: *What if she was right*, you'd think, *what if I am sick?* Slowly, over time, you'd keep coming back to the idea, late at night, when your mind was roaming. *What if I am sick?* you'd think. And every time you had that thought, it would be a little bit of water to the seed of the idea, until eventually you would become truly unwell.'

'But why would you want a powder that does that?'

'I wanted to warn people against the ideas that they take on board about themselves.'

'Still,' said Victor. 'That seems like a bad invention.'

'It is,' said Polina. 'And it was never supposed to be let loose like that.'

'But how are we supposed to cure them if they're not really sick?'

'That's easy, we give them medicine that isn't really medicine.' Polina dug around in her bag and produced a couple of white pills. 'These are nothing but sugar,' she explained. 'But if we promise your parents they're a cure, then they'll be cured. The pain came from their heads and the cure shall come from their heads too.'

Back in the bedroom, Polina announced to Victor's parents that she was a doctor and had come to them with a cure for the sickness that plagued them.

Both parents swallowed the sugar pills.

Ten minutes later, they were as fit and healthy as they'd

ever been, and they pulled their son into a bear hug, and their eyes were shining.

Polina watched their reunion with a quiet happiness. Once it was over, she put a hand on Victor's shoulder. 'I'm glad your parents are well again,' she whispered. 'But don't let them get too happy. You forget, Walter Swizwit and the collectors from the dark fortress are still on their way.'

35

Once everyone in Rainwater had been cured, they all gathered together beside a roaring bonfire that tore a huge orange strip out of the night sky.

The people of the four villages introduced themselves to each other.

They traded stories of monsters and angels.

They feasted on bowls of sweet oats.

Huge vats of sweet tea were made and drunk.

Songs were sung, dances were danced.

The people felt relief for the first time in many weeks. Even after Polina had explained that the collectors would still be hunting them, the mood remained lively.

In a quiet corner, Victor sat between his parents, recounting the adventures he'd had over the last couple of weeks.

'I found Saint Oswald,' said Mingus, bounding over to

them with the tortoise in his hands. Saint Oswald, who hadn't realised she'd needed finding in the first place, rolled her eyes at the boy who was holding her.

'Who is this?' asked Victor's dad.

'This is Mingus,' said Victor. 'And that's Mo-Lan, and Elena.'

The three of them took it in turns to shake Victor's parents' hands.

'Wonderful to meet you all!' said Victor's dad. 'We're so glad Victor's made friends!'

'Thank you for looking after my boy,' said his mum.

'Actually,' said Elena, 'he kind of looked after us.'

'Shhh,' said Mo-Lan, pointing over her shoulder. 'The big lady's going to speak.'

The Great Aunt stood beside the fire and addressed the gathering with a heavy mug of tea clasped between her hands.

'So,' she said. 'Something has brought us together and together we are. We welcome you, folk from the villages of Moonwald, Aeldbird and Sektun-Layley.'

The villagers around the fire clapped.

'It might be a struggle, but we shall find places for you all. Our home is now your home. Over the coming weeks and months, we shall build new accommodations for you all, and make sure that every person who wants it has work and food. It is an awful thing, to lose your home, but it is a great one to make new friends.'

The villagers cheered.

'Now, it has come to my attention that some of you are not aware of how to plant seeds, spin wool or blow glass.'

The villagers laughed.

'That is something we shall have to fix. We will teach you these things and in return we will look forward to learning from you. There . . .'

Her speech trailed off as a shabby old wagon manned by two riders in black cloaks burst out of the forest and tottered into the centre of the gathering.

It came to a halt.

The villagers jumped to their feet, ready to launch an attack.

They stopped when they realised that the rider was not alone. All around Rainwater, soldiers sat on horseback, their hands resting on the swords that hung by their sides. They were surrounded and outnumbered.

Victor felt the breath catch in his throat. Was this really it? he thought. They'd finally managed to get back to his home and all he'd had was a few moments with his parents.

The rider tossed back the hood of his cloak.

It was Walter Swizwit.

'You're a collector?' asked Victor, stepping forward.

'Of course I'm not a collector,' said Walter Swizwit, who was breathing so heavily it sounded like he'd just run up a thousand stairs.

'Then what are you doing here?'

'That was what I'd been trying to tell you, except you kept running every time we got close to you. You people,' he said, shaking his head. 'Why won't you sit still for a second? I only needed to talk. We almost had you and then you vanished into that godforsaken mine.'

Walter Swizwit nudged his horse toward the Great Aunt. 'I see you're in charge,' he said. 'And I've come to offer my help.'

'Why would we talk to you?' she spat. 'It's because of you that we've all been sick as dogs for weeks.'

'You've gotten me wrong. I can't say I blame you, and I understand completely that you would be furious with me, but I'm certain you'll want to hear what I have to say.'

None of the villagers were impressed. They didn't believe him. Why would they? He'd told them nothing but lies and done them nothing but harm.

'No one's going to offer me a cup of tea then?' he asked, half-joking.

They weren't.

'All right,' he said. 'I understand. But at least allow me to tell you my story.'

'Keep it short,' said the Great Aunt. 'There's no love for you here. We have defences to get up and new houses to build.'

Walter Swizwit jumped off his horse.

He knelt down and wiped the sweat from his forehead. In the flickering light of the fire, he told his story.

'Years ago,' he said, 'I lived in a little wooden house with my little sister. It had been a while since our parents had passed on but they'd taught us how to live alongside the land and we had a good, simple life. We planted a variety of crops and every year we took them to market in the nearest town, selling them for enough to get through the coming months.

'One year, our crops failed. Not just one of them, but every single grain and vegetable we'd planted. It was as though someone had poisoned the very ground from which they grew. Without the money I'd make selling our crops in the market, I knew we wouldn't have enough to get through the year.

'That was when the collector rode in on his horse.

'He offered to loan us the money in exchange for paying him back a little every year from then on. Me and my sister had a long and heated argument. In the end, we decided that we had no other choice. We accepted his deal.

'But the next year, our crops failed again, and we had nothing with which to pay back the collector. So the collector brought in a group of riders and they took my little sister away as payment.

'I did nothing. Absolutely nothing. While they carried away what was left of my family, I stood frozen by the empty barn. I was young, I was afraid. I had none of the courage that my sister had.

'In the years after that, I travelled around living off the land. Sometimes I stole chickens to eat or traded fruits and nuts I'd gathered in the woods. I slept wherever I could. I never felt like finding somewhere to settle down. I couldn't face trying to build a new home. All that time, I felt a fury growing in me. At first, it was a fury at myself for doing nothing, and then it was a fury at the collectors for intruding on our peaceful lives. If they hadn't come by, we would have managed, I know we would have. It would have been tough, but we'd always gotten by before.

'And then I got on a ferry bound for the Old West. I'd been told there was some work there and I was getting tired of this side of the ocean; it held too many memories. That was when I met old Polina and stole her magnificent inventions.

'By selling her inventions all across the seven hills, I was raising money for an army that could take on the collectors. I wanted to crush them so that I could free my sister and make sure they would never again have power over the people of this land. But I lost my way. Something about having money ate up my mind. The more I had, the more I wanted, and the more I devoted myself to making money, the less space I had in my head for anything else. I am ashamed to say that I all but forgot about my sister.'

Walter Swizwit looked as though he was about to cry.

'And then,' he said, turning to the four children, 'I went chasing after your children once they escaped my dungeon. But somehow, your clever kids had managed to free the prisoners of the collectors, and I could once again hug my sister outside the gates of their dark fortress.'

At that, the other person on the wagon jumped off and tipped back the hood of her cloak. Victor recognised the woman's face from the photo he'd glimpsed back at Walter's castle in Kaftan Minor.

'It was then that I realised what a grave mistake I had made,' said the pedlar. 'It was then that I hurried to raise the army I'd once planned and rushed here with my sister to fight alongside you.'

For a moment, the people of the four villages were silent.

'You still poisoned us,' said the Great Aunt. 'Even if you had been trying to raise money for an army.'

'And all I can do is apologise,' said Walter Swizwit. 'I am a thousand miles from perfect and there are times when my anger turns me ugly. All I ask now is that you let me stand and fight in your village.'

'He's always been an idiot and he's not even the greatest inventor in our family,' said Walter Swizwit's sister, stepping out of his shadow. 'But he's not a bad person really.'

'Do we have a choice but to let you fight with us?' asked the Great Aunt.

'You do, of course. I could meet them in the forest, though they are better riders than us and know the paths better, so they would have an advantage. If you let us fight from Rainwater, we'll have a far better chance of victory.'

The Great Aunt turned back to the people.

In the light of the fire, her gnarled face looked like it was made of ancient stone. She seemed like a being that had existed since the dawn of time.

'We do not want any blood shed on the ground of our home,' she said. 'But there is only so far you can run until your back is against a wall. All we can do is promise that our doors remain open for anyone who does not wish to fight.' She raised her voice so that the soldiers waiting around the village would hear. 'If any of you should decide to put down your weapons,' she shouted, 'you will be welcome to take shelter in our homes.' She turned around and spoke to the forest too. 'That goes for you lot as well!' she shouted.

'Who is she talking to?' Victor whispered to Elena.

'Them,' Elena whispered back, pointing to the line of trees.

There, hundreds of collectors took one step out of the gloom. They stood perfectly still at the border between the village and the forest. The wind riffled their black cloaks like flags. Victor could see snatches of their pale blue hands, and the gleam of their swords as they drew them from their sheaths.

Victor shuddered with fright.

He gripped Elena's hand.

Mo-Lan closed her eyes.

And Mingus took Saint Oswald back in his arms.

'Quickly!' ordered the Great Aunt. 'Everyone back to their houses. Lock your doors and cover your windows. We are battening the hatches until terror is gone from this place.'

36

For three days and three nights, the pedlar's army faced off against the forces of the collectors. They did not ride straight at each other. Instead, they watched and waited.

At night, stray arrows whistled through the air.

And swords clanged as they were sharpened.

But no fighting took place.

Not yet.

The collectors were gathering their forces. Every hour that passed, more of them arrived to reinforce the waiting army. They had never faced an enemy as strong as the pedlar's army and they wanted to be sure they would not lose. There was too much at stake.

The houses of Moonwald were packed. Four villages had been squashed into one. People lay under tables, in barns, on kitchen floors and in corridors.

People lay everywhere but hardly anyone slept.

The days and nights were tense with fright. A fragile quiet fell over Rainwater. It was a quiet filled with rustles and hushed whispers.

But in those anxious days and nights, Victor learned something about his parents: while he'd been away, they'd learned how to make time go by. Where once they had filled their days with nothing but work, now they laughed and joked with each other like a pair of clowns.

'What happened to you two?' he asked them one afternoon.

'We had a lot of nothing to do in that bed,' his mother said. 'And we realised just how wonderful that was. Time is going to pass us by, no matter what we do. It'll turn us old and slow and wrinkly. While it passes, we can either scowl at it and shake our fists, or wave at it and smile.' She grinned at Victor. 'We know we were too focused on work and we're sorry. We're going to make room for the rest of life, if those vile collectors ever go away.'

'Does this mean I won't have to do chores any more?' Victor asked hopefully.

His dad laughed. 'It means you'll sing as you scrub! Smile as you clean! Laugh as you work the field!'

Victor shook his head. 'I think you're both still sick,' he said.

'I think you're fun,' said Mingus, beaming.

The two gleeful adults forced the four children to play games they'd invented. They put on plays, invented limericks and set traps around the houses, roaring whenever anyone fell into one. While the soldiers faced off with the collectors, Victor's house was filled with laughter.

At night, the children whispered to each other before falling asleep.

'Is everyone asleep?' Mingus would ask from under the bed.

'No,' Victor would reply from the hammock.

'Yes,' Elena would say from the bed.

'Shhhh,' Mo-Lan would whisper from the rug by the fire.

'I'm sorry about your villages,' said Victor, on the third night of the stand-off.

'Wasn't your fault,' said Elena.

'And this is home now,' said Mingus.

'Shhh,' whispered Mo-Lan. 'Some of us are trying to sleep.'

37

A t the edges of the village, Walter Swizwit and Polina
sat on the grass staring out at the swelling forces of
the collectors.

'There are ten times as many of them as there are of you,'
said Polina.

'Then we'll have to fight ten times as hard,' said Walter
Swizwit.

'It will all be for nothing.'

The pedlar spat on the ground. 'What else is there to do?'
he asked. 'These people have already lost their homes and
those savages waiting in the trees will have their souls once
they get their claws on them.'

'You'll fail.'

'Do you have a better idea?'

Polina nodded. 'Give me your wagon,' she said.

Walter Swizwit laughed. 'What'll you do with my old

wagon?' he said.

'Wait and see,' said Polina.

The pedlar rolled his eyes. 'You have a funny mind,' he said. 'But it works a whole lot better than mine. You can take my wagon, as long as you don't lose it.'

'How do you lose a wagon?'

'If you stop paying attention, you could even lose yourself. That's what happened to me.' He eyed the ground in embarrassment. 'That's why I did what I did to you, and I'm sorry.'

*

In the deepest hour of the night, Polina rode into the forest. She rode silently, with a black cape covering her head. Carefully, she slipped between the ranks of the waiting collectors. She passed the camps they'd set up all along the line of the trees, with blazing fires and roasting pigs and great wooden buckets hung to catch the rain for drinking water.

She shivered as she caught sight of the enemy. They were spindly, bony things, that breathed blue clouds and barely spoke to each other. They ate alone, huddled against trees. When they slept, they roared in their dreams. A smell of rotten fruit clung to them like a fog.

Carefully, Polina guided the clanking wagon around the dank encampments.

'Go gently, girl,' she whispered to the horse. 'That's it.'

She trembled with fear.

After what felt like years, the real inventor passed the sickly collectors. She found the main path through the forest and asked her horse to pick up speed. Together they galloped onwards. Slowly, Polina felt the warmth returning to her fingers.

38

In the first hours of the stand-off's twenty-first morning, the sky split open and rain began to fall over the village of Rainwater.

It was a drizzly, grey day where you could barely see your hand in front of your face.

The sun covered its face with grumbling clouds.

No one saw a raggedy plane, fixed to a balloon, as it chugged through the messy sky. And no one saw the pilot of that plane throwing her own strange inventions out of the back of it.

As they woke, the collectors found themselves surrounded by Mirrors of Emit Tsol, Greengrass Stereoscopes and Moveable Worlds. Having spent so long doing things they hated, every one of them immediately latched on to the new methods of escaping from the world. Some of them sat blinking open-mouthed at their own reflections. Others stared, hypnotised, into the small wooden binoculars that showed people far happier than they had ever been. And some sat with model farms in their laps, moving tiny sheep and cows around tiny paddocks.

At first, the High Count stalked among his collectors, bellowing for them to put down the inventions. But it was too late. They were already lost. And pretty soon, the count himself picked up a Greengrass Stereoscope, and found himself completely immersed in the lives of people that had never existed.

And that was how the collectors were finally defeated.

Not in a great battle, but with a set of inventions that had once caused great pain.

Polina sighed as she saw it unfold below the stormy clouds. It seemed that her inventions had found a use after all. She brought her plane low and watched in fascination as collector after collector succumbed to the spell of her three unusual contraptions.

In that moment, Polina realised that being a great inventor was not just about creating something amazing, but about finding a way of using that creation to make the world a better place.

Meanwhile, Walter Swizwit ran between the houses of Rainwater, knocking on doors and yelling that it was safe to come out. The people trickled out of their houses.

'Is it really safe?' they asked.

It was.

They danced in the rain until their lips turned blue.

On hearing that the collectors had been defeated, people came from far and wide to plunder the dark fortress for everything that they had lost in the years since the Iron Plague. Greenbeard and the rest of the relatives who had been waiting for their loved ones left the forest and returned to their villages. They were no longer the people in the trees. In fact, it was the collectors who spent the rest of their lives high in the canopy, where they could while away their hours on Polina's inventions without being disturbed.

39

Every morning, Victor was woken by a giant tortoise nibbling on his little toe. The name of the tortoise was Saint Oswald. The name of the town in which Victor lived was Rainwater and it sat at the bottom of a valley, surrounded by three snow-capped mountains and one dark forest.

'Get off,' he'd tell the giant tortoise.

'*Uk, uk,*' the giant tortoise would reply.

Together they would race to the top of the smallest mountain and look out over their home. Victor liked being there when the sun rose. It meant he could watch as his town slowly came to life. Windows flew open, smoke puffed from chimneys and the streets began to fill up.

If Victor ever felt small or alone, he only had to head up to the mountain, and from there he could see that he was part of something much bigger than himself.

Rainwater was four times the size it once had been. It had windmills now, and towering buildings, and winding streets of cobble long enough for you to get lost in. It had a bakery that leaked the sweet smell of fresh pastries into the morning. It had a school and a shop and a library so big that you could never even come close to finishing all the books on its shelves. Rainwater even had a tiny train that linked it to Kaftan Minor, the further cities and the ocean that faced the Old West.

How had they done it?

The miners had found coal in the mountains, which the scientists had used to power all kinds of machines. The hunters, on the other hand, had given up hunting to become doctors and writers and builders and actors. Most people in Rainwater couldn't guess in the morning where they'd end up by the afternoon. There were still certain boring things that needed to be done, that was true, but when they were done, everyone was free to do as they wished.

Once the sun was up, Victor and Saint Oswald would trip back down the mountain to their house. They'd wolf down breakfast and dash out to meet their friends Elena, Mingus and Mo-Lan in the fields.

'What shall we do today?' Victor would ask each morning.

'Whatever we want to do,' would come the answer.

With his story done, the boy stood up. The blue light of morning was falling in from outside. We both walked to the window and found that it had stopped snowing.

'You should be all right to head back now,' he said. 'The tortoise will take you; make sure you don't get lost.'

'Thanks for the story,' I said, and I stuck out my hand to shake his.

The boy ignored my hand and drew me into a hug. 'Thanks for not robbing our house when you had the chance,' he said.

'You're welcome,' I told him. I didn't say it, but to be honest, I don't think there was anything in the house that would have been worth robbing.

Before I left, I turned around. 'Are you okay out here?' I asked. 'Do you need anything?'

'I'm okay,' the boy promised. 'My parents will be back tomorrow. They've just gone to visit their friend. She's an inventor.'

I breathed a sigh of relief. At least he had parents. 'Would you mind if I told people your story?'

'Do whatever you like with it,' the boy said. 'It's not mine anyway; Dad told it to me.'

The giant tortoise led me calmly through the rising light of the woods. Every now and again, it would turn its head back to check I was still following. I would wave to the giant tortoise.

'*Uk, uk,*' it would say.

When we eventually reached the main road, the tortoise came to a stop and refused to move any farther. It gestured with its head for me to go on.

I knelt down to say goodbye.

'Well,' I said. 'Thank you very much for rescuing me. If it wasn't for you, I'd probably have frozen solid two nights ago.'

'*Uk, uk,*' said the tortoise, toodling back the way we'd come.

I walked alongside the road. The air was so cold it burned my chest when I breathed. Two houses came into view, along with a street light that had just blinked off. It was a relief.

Back at the old wooden house, I made a huge pot of coffee and settled down with a thick pad of paper. I made myself promise not to touch the computer. It couldn't help me, I knew that. All it could do was distract me from what I wanted to be doing.

Then I wrote.

And wrote.

And wrote.

At ten o'clock, I lit a fire, made another coffee and ate fourteen chocolate chip cookies. Then I got back to the writing. This went on for three days. For three days and three nights, I wrote, drank coffee, ate cookies and stared into the fire. Not once did I touch my computer. Sometimes my belly moaned that it wanted something other than cookies. I'll give you some vegetables later, I told it, I've got more important things to do right now.

When the three days were up, I blinked tiredly at the morning sun.

The morning sun stared back at me.

Look, I told it. I wrote a story.

NOTES

🔘 All tortoises are turtles, but not all turtles are tortoises. The term 'turtle' actually covers over two hundred different kinds of tortoises, turtles, and terrapins. Although all tortoises live only on the land, so do certain types of turtle.

🔘 It can be quite difficult to tell the difference between male and female tortoises. As Polina explains, the shape of the stomach can be a clue, as can the size of the tails (males' are bigger) and notches on the bottom of their shells (females tend to have U-shaped notches, while males are more likely to have V-shaped notches).

🔘 Saint Oswald is named after an old English king who ruled Northumbria from the year 634 until his death in 641. He's buried in my hometown, Gloucester.

🔘 Researchers have found that if you're holding a warm drink while talking to someone, you're more likely to see them in a friendly light. There are also types of tea, like chamomile, that have been shown to help people calm down.

Stereoscopes first became popular in the mid 1800s. As travel was extremely expensive, many people used them as ways of experiencing distant landscapes, landmarks, and people.

The average British person spends a total of fifty days per year looking at a screen. I'm still trying to cut down.

ACKNOWLEDGEMENTS

I am hugely grateful to Nuoren Voiman Liitto for the Villa Sarkia Residency, where this book was written. Thank you also to the people of Sysmä, Finland. And thank you to Mark for the food, karaoke, and company.

Thank you, again, to Tig, who turned this from half a story into a whole one. Thanks to Ruth and everyone else at Quercus for another adventure. Thanks to George for the wonderful illustrations. Thanks to Matthew for doing the grown-up stuff.

Lastly but not leastly, thanks as always to Renata, Beth, and Nan.

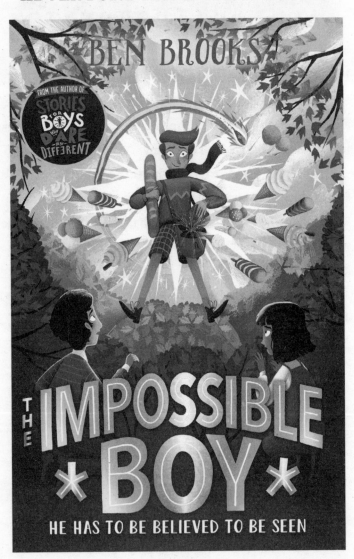